A Romantic Mystery
NOVEL

Shadow of Doubt

DIANE K. TODD

ACCENT BOOKS

Accent Books™ is an imprint of David C. Cook Publishing Co.
David C. Cook Publishing Co., Elgin, Illinois 60120
David C. Cook Publishing Co., Weston, Ontario
Nova Distribution Ltd., Newton Abbot, England

SHADOW OF DOUBT
©1992 by Diane K. Todd

Cover design by Turnbaugh & Associates
Cover Illustration by Kevin Bielfus
First Printing, 1992
Printed in the United States of America
96 95 94 93 92 5 4 3 2 1

Library of Congress Catalog Card Number 91-72851

ISBN 0-7814-0947-0

This book is dedicated to my father,
David Renaud Halblom.

– 1 –

"...tyre—come to the information desk. Miss Lissa McIntyre, the information desk, please."

Lissa moved through the crowd of bustling airline travelers. Shifting the strap of her camera tote, she eased the pressure on her shoulder as she rounded the corner to the information desk. "I'm Lissa McIntyre."

The woman behind the counter smiled. "There's a telephone call for you, Miss McIntyre. Over here."

Lissa spoke her thanks and brushed back tickling wisps of hair that had escaped her loosely twisted blonde knot. She lifted the receiver to her ear.

"Hello."

"Lissa...it's Karl."

"Karl! This is *great!* Where are you? How did you find me at the airport, of all places?"

"I need you to do something for me."

Lissa's tone changed to a good-natured reprimand. "Don't tell me I'm going to be your errand girl again. The last time

I did that I ended up on a merry goose chase that entirely destroyed my afternoon...and I had work to do, too."

"I'll make it up to you—"

"I could like that idea...say, dinner at...Ricardo's? Tonight, before you tell me you have to leave. That will make up for being gone so long this time. We'll discuss retribution for my wasted afternoon later."

"Lissa...."

Lissa stopped short. "What?"

"Would you just *listen*?"

An odd gasp came to Lissa's ears. "Karl...?" There was a drawn-out hiss, followed by a sigh, then, carefully, Lissa asked, "What's going on? Where are you?"

"Do you remember how we used to play Resistance?"

Lissa frowned. It was a child's game they had played as children—a spy game, cloak and dagger type.

"I remember."

"Play it with me."

"What?" Lissa rejected the urge to look over her shoulder. She hesitated. "If this is a joke, Karl, I think you've strung it along far enough."

"I wish...it were a joke...or...at the very least...a bad dream. I have a key I need you to keep until I decide what to do with it. I can't...trust anyone else. This is *very important*," he hissed when Lissa tried to interrupt him. *"Please* listen. I have only you to turn to."

Her fingers drifted to her throat. She felt the deep beating of her heart. "All right. I'm listening."

"I'm here at the airport...in the last phone booth on the right."

Lissa sharply checked the shift of her gaze.

Resistance. Never let the enemy know where your contact is located.

"Okay. What do you want me to do?"

Karl's voice carried a strange, deliberate quality. "I am

6

going to leave the key...in the change receptacle of this telephone. I need you to take it and keep it for me." Karl drew a sharp, choked breath. "I'll stay in the phone booth after you hang up...just to the point...the point where you can be certain no one else will enter the booth before you can get to it. Do you understand what I'm saying?"

"Yes, but—"

"Don't argue. I can't expla..."

"Karl, what is it?"

"Someone...Lissa, don't trust anyone," Karl's voice sharpened. "Not *anyone*." His voice strained, seemed to crack. "I'll contact you as soon as I can."

"Karl, *please*...."

The receiver buzzed in Lissa's ear. Staring at it for a moment in disbelief, she dropped it into its cradle. Uncertain, Lissa turned casually and scanned the room to see a man—Karl—in the phone booth, as he said. He wore a denim jacket with the collar up. He stood facing the wall.

With a furtive look about her, Lissa hoisted her purse and camera case to her shoulder. Her head buzzed. People who earlier had given off a friendly, busy feeling now seemed to reach out in suspicion. The man who glanced her way...the woman with the tan coat who was staring at her...the uniformed security guard.

Lissa's heart pounded as she stopped a few feet from the row of telephone booths. Some were occupied, others were not. Lissa paused as if to search for change...or a telephone number...anything to allow a reasonable excuse to give Karl time to leave.

Karl was not moving.

Lissa fumbled with some change. She attempted to stay calm and look uncertain.

Finally, making a move to leave the tiny cubicle, Karl rested a hand briefly against the doors after shoving them out of his way. The other hand he slid stiffly into his jacket pocket.

Lissa nearly voiced her shock. Karl was scraggly, unkempt, haggard. His dark hair was long, and he had grown a beard since she had last seen him. Yet, it was his eyes that filled Lissa with disbelief. Dark hollows of fierce blue sank into drawn features. His face was a sickly yellow beneath the weathered bronze of his skin.

Something was terribly, horribly wrong.

"Excuse me," she said suddenly as Karl started to turn away. "Do you have change for a dollar?"

For a moment Lissa thought Karl was going to ignore her. Then she thought he might collapse where he stood. Karl swayed as he stopped. His jaw tensed. Through the intense impact of his gaze, Lissa stayed still, not moving to keep him from falling.

"Sure, lady," Karl replied huskily, slipping his free hand into the pocket of his jeans. "Here," he dropped some coins into her palm. His fingers barely grazed her skin, but they were burning with fever. "Keep it," he muttered as she tried to offer her own dollar in return.

"Thanks," Lissa said to Karl's back as he dipped his head and shuffled in the other direction. She forced herself to look away from his brave attempt not to stagger.

What was Karl doing?

What was going on?

Lissa maneuvered herself into the phone booth and closed the door against the noise around her. She stood for a moment in the muted silence, hardly daring to believe what was happening.

Karl...was ill. That much was obvious. And she...she was playing Resistance?

Be normal. Always act as if you are doing just what people expect you to do.

Remembering the look on Karl's face, Lissa gave a shudder of fear; this was no game.

Lissa sifted through the coins Karl had given her and dropped the correct amount into the slot. She pushed buttons, the beeps of her own telephone number sounding in her ear. The telephone rang twice, afterward connecting to her answering machine. With a sense of lost reality, Lissa heard her own bubbling voice explain that she was unable to answer the call at the present and to, "Please leave your name and number, and I'll get back to you as soon as I possibly can."

She could not believe she was hearing herself say, "This is Lissa. I'm back in town and I'll try calling later."

Lissa replaced the receiver and listened to the machine swallow her coins. She plunged her index finger into the change receptacle. She could feel the key, still warm from Karl's fevered hand. Sliding it out into her hand, Lissa shoved her fist into the pocket of her slacks without looking at the object.

She had it.

But what was it for?

Taking a deep breath to calm her racing heart, Lissa opened the door. She shifted her bags on her shoulder with her free hand as she stepped into the moving crowd of people. Her gaze darted back and forth, but she saw nothing suspicious.

What would she look for, anyway?

What had Karl gotten her into? What had he done?

What is going on, Lord? she prayed. *Help me. I don't understand all this.*

Lissa walked toward the luggage area, her fingers clenching the key in her pocket. Most of the luggage from her incoming flight had already been retrieved. A few pieces, including her two, waited on the silent carousel. A group of businessmen, talking of meetings to happen, were moving away. A small boy came running past and snared a red bag, only to dash, laughing, back toward his mother. The woman caught him in her arms and turned to walk the other direction.

Lissa stepped toward her closest bag and took hold of it with her left hand. Rounding the far side of the carousel, she saw a man walking toward her.

Lissa fought the unexpected urge to bolt and run. Her hand clutched the key tighter.

The man's face was lean and masculine. Vertical lines etched the sides of his mouth. Creased lines radiated from the corners of his eyes. He gave her a perfunctory smile. The fact that it was merely an automatic reaction did not diminish the sense of nervous fear that pulsated through Lissa.

Such unusual eyes. They were...brown lightened with streaks of blue...and a touch of gray.

The man shot her another look, this time a closer inspection, and Lissa realized she had been staring.

Flustered by the sharpness of his gaze, Lissa jerked her hand from her pocket to snatch at her remaining piece of luggage...and the key went flying through the air to bounce, tinging, several feet away.

For one horrified moment both of them stood still. The man's look went from Lissa to the key. He turned and bent to retrieve it. Looking up from the small bronze object on his fingers, the man asked, "Did you cut yourself?"

"Did I...?" Lissa started. Her eyes widened as she glanced at her hand.

Her fingertips were smeared with blood.

- 2 -

The man was waiting.

"I...I," Lissa stopped, her heart pounding. She swallowed and drew as deep a breath as she dared, attempting to still the roaring that had begun in her head. She knew she had not cut herself.

Resistance.

Lissa set her baggage down and made a show of rummaging through her purse for a tissue.

"Here," the man said, reaching into his suit jacket pocket. "Take this." He handed her a clean handkerchief.

Lissa shook her head. "I couldn't. I'd...I really don't need it."

"Looks like you do," the man replied. He accompanied his comment with a dry shadow of a smile, lifting the folded cloth toward her.

Lissa took it, if only to appease the man...and to have something to wrap around her fingers before he realized the blood was not her own. Twisting the handkerchief about her hand, Lissa tucked the loose ends under to keep them in place.

"Thank you," she said, to which he replied a distinct, "You're welcome," and produced another handkerchief which he used to wipe the key clean before returning it to her. "I'm from a large family," he gave as explanation for the extra handkerchief as he scrubbed at the slight stains remaining on his thumb. "I never broke the habit of taking an extra along for one of my kid sisters."

"Me, too...from a large family, I mean," Lissa added, a bit disjointed. "I've got five brothers."

The man said, "I've got three sisters."

Lissa was quiet, not knowing what to say. She returned the key to her pocket and reached for her luggage.

"Let me help," he offered, bending to retrieve her largest piece.

"I can manage."

"It's no bother."

Lissa steadied her purse and camera case, then bent to lift the smaller of her two bags.

"Is this all?" The man's expression was sharply observant. Lissa nodded. He asked, "Are you meeting someone or should I call a taxi?"

"Meeting someone?" Lissa repeated, her gaze flickering at, then away from the man. "No. No, I'm not." He was watching her again. "My car...is in the parking lot."

Automatic sliding glass doors whooshed open as they approached them. The evening was cool with the smell of autumn dampness in the air.

"My name is Brent Jamison."

"Lissa McIntyre."

"Do you live in town, Miss McIntyre?"

"Yes."

They walked past rows of parked cars.

"For very long?"

12

"The last three years."

"I see you like to take pictures....Your camera case," he indicated, when her head swiveled toward him in surprise.

"Yes. I take pictures."

"And I ask too many questions. Sorry. Part of my business," he added with a shrug.

Lissa refrained from asking just what sort of business that was.

"This is my car." Lissa said, placing her baggage on the concrete behind her Eagle Talon. The man put the suitcase he carried alongside it.

"Thank you, Mr. Jamison, for your assistance. I think I can take care of it from here."

"My pleasure, Miss McIntyre." Brent Jamison tipped his head slightly in acknowledgment. His brownish-blue eyes studied her for a moment longer than she liked, then he turned and walked back toward the airport. Lissa watched the easy swing of his stride putting distance between the two of them. He raised his hand at a taxi, disappeared into the vehicle, and was gone.

Lissa realized her hands were trembling. As long as she held her luggage, she could mask the faint quaking. However, now, as she stared at the taxi driving away, the shaking became more pronounced.

Grasping one hand tightly with the other, Lissa stood still for several seconds. A fertile imagination, bred from years of playing a child's game, had her suspicious and jumpy. Brent Jamison was unimportant. Their meeting was purely coincidental. He had drawn the logical conclusion regarding the blood on the key.

A spurt of fear shot through her. Karl must be badly hurt! But how badly? Where was he now?

Managing to insert her key into the lock on the hatch, she popped open the lid and placed her luggage inside. The hatchback snicked shut.

She stood still, hands on the back of the car. She had never seen eyes quite like Brent Jamison's. Terribly unusual...and penetrating. Lissa shook herself to clear her mind of those eyes. The leather car seat folded around her as she got in. The taxi with Brent Jamison was long gone.

Fortunately, the drive home was quick and didn't require great concentration.

Lissa's apartment complex was new, located in quiet surroundings with extra amenities she rarely took time to enjoy.

Shuddering a sigh of relief, Lissa kicked her apartment door shut behind her. For a moment she absorbed the elegant, easy style of her home. The comfortable, airy look was done in pastels and cream, warmed now by the late rays of the sun thrusting shafts of sunlight through the vertical blinds covering the sliding doors of her living room.

Lissa dropped her luggage in a pile beside the door.

She was at a loss. Other than commit a key to her and warn her against trusting anyone else, Karl had failed to give her any instructions...or explanations.

Lissa swiped at the loose tendrils of hair tickling her cheeks. What could have caused Karl's injury? She pulled two enameled pins from her hair knot as she stepped through the living room. Curls of blonde hair tumbled back over her shoulders. She gave them an absentminded, finger-raking shake to loosen the twist. The pins were laid on the kitchen bar. Next to them she placed the key. Lissa's palms flattened on the counter; the key and the pins lay between the space of her hands. What was she supposed to do now? Just wait?

Lissa stared at the key, wiped clean from any hint of stain. It was small and brass. There was nothing unusual about it.

Lord, I'm uneasy. I don't know what's happened to Karl. You know he's always been one to find trouble, and I don't know what sort of problem he's gotten himself into this time, but I know he needs your help. She was still. *So do I. He*

14

wants me to keep this key...and I don't know what it's for. I need your wisdom, Father. I'm afraid...for Karl...for me. Please show me what I'm supposed to do. I ask it in your Son Jesus' name.

Lissa's gaze lifted from the counter top to rest on her answering machine. Eyes widening, she began to wonder.... Could it be possible....

Of course! If Karl could not talk in person, he could have left a message on the machine.

Lissa's fingers stretched toward the answering machine to press the play switch.

At that moment the telephone rang, a quietly shrill sound that abruptly stilled her movements.

– 3 –

Lissa stared at the telephone. When it rang again, she grabbed it. Her greeting was a breathless, "Hi."

Cynthia, her business partner, sang back, "Hi! You're home! We missed you. How was your trip? And the wedding? Why didn't you call or drop by? I've got a ton of things to ask you." She laughed. "You can imagine the things I want you to look at." Her topic altered with a half breath and an imagined pause, "Julie says Karl Karello called."

"Karl?"

"He called once...no," a half-space of time, "two times. Lissa, you really should just nab that man, you know. Permanently. He's adorable. At least if you two were an item, you'd know where to get a hold of each other."

Cynthia stopped to take a complete breath, which was just long enough for Lissa to ask, "When did he call the last time?"

"I don't know. A couple hours ago? I told him you were

16

flying in from Colorado and gave him your arrival time. He acted like he'd meet you at the airport."

"Did he say what he wanted?"

Cynthia laughed, a delicate trill of amusement full of implication. "What more could he want but to see you? Seriously, Lissa," Cynthia continued, "are you coming down? Julie and Donny are here. *Temporarily*, they say. If you're much later, they've threatened to make you wait until tomorrow to see their jubilant faces. Actually, they'll stay," she amended. "We're sorta backlogged here. Not bad. We're catching up. But can you bring us something to eat? The refrigerator is *empty* and I can think of only one reason why it could be: Donny. I'm glad I'm not that kid's mother!"

"Something to eat? Yes, I'll bring something." Lissa's face twisted. "But Karl...he didn't say anything more?"

"Just that he'd try to see you at the airport. Could you hurry? You know how Donny can be when he gets hungry...which is *always*!" She inserted an aside to the voices in the background, then "Donny'd like pizza. I'm for some chicken. Better make it pizza, though. Donny's threatening me." There was laughter.

Lissa could visualize the display of exuberant teenage body language accompanying the additional comments in the background.

Cynthia added, "I'll call in the order to Izzi's. You can pick it up on the way here. Okay?"

"Fine. It sounds fine. Give me an extra fifteen minutes before you call the order in. I need to change clothes and listen to my answering machine."

"You got it. See you in a little while. Bye!"

Lissa dearly loved Cynthia, but *sometimes*....

Her fingers tripped the play button on her answering machine. There was an assortment of messages, then....

"Ah, the sound of your voice—like a hint of fresh breeze, it is."

Lissa's heart skipped a beat. *Karl.* "I'm home. At least for the time being, anyway. I've missed your company and our spirited discussions. This last trip was grueling, but I've good news to share. It'll take my mind off all the junk that's happening in the world before my editor—the slave driver—expects me out again. I'm safe for the time being, though. He's on vacation. I need a vacation," there was a sigh, "but all I have is three days, then it's off to Europe this time before I swing through Israel to cover what I can before I come home again. Sometimes I think I should quit this business, but," she could visualize the crooked swing of his smile and the gleam in his blue eyes, "you know me. Get home," he continued, "so I can quit talking to this machine and talk with you face to face. I've some wonderfully exciting news to share."

The tape recorded a click and hum. Two more calls with trivial messages followed. The third call was Karl.

"Lissa...me again. Julie, your loyal and fervent receptionist, has informed me you are out of town until tomorrow. So," he shifted topics, "elder brother Jake decided it was time to tie the knot. Too bad I wasn't there to witness the nuptials. I'm off to take a few shots of local interest, besides investigate a story lead on an overseas connection I've been working on. I'll call later...or you can call me. I do want to see you before I have to leave. I've got things to tell you." Karl hung up.

That was all?

She heard the sound of her own voice saying, "...I'll try calling later." Then, suddenly, unexpectedly, another message started.

"Lissa, I can't go home."

Karl!

She gave a quick gasp and strained to hear the words. Karl paused. She could hear the thunder of traffic noise, then his coarse, accelerated breathing. "They'll follow me.

They've been...following me. Whatever you do, be careful. Don't trust anyone. I'll try to keep in touch. Pray for me." A soft noise filled her ears. More breathing. His voice became whispery, colored with regret. "I've really done it this time." A pause. "I don't think I ever told you...how much I have...always appreciated you."

"Oh, *Karl*," Lissa breathed as his last syllables whispered over the static. "What's happened to you?"

There was a clatter. The connection severed. The tape lapsed into silence, clicked, hummed as it rewound.

Lissa stared at the answering machine. Her focus changed to the key Karl had given her.

Resistance.

Karl was counting on her.

But what did he expect her to do?

How was she going to find him? She *had* to find him. Karl was hurt. He needed help.

Taking the key, Lissa strode through the rooms, hurrying to her bedroom. She rattled back her closet doors and pulled out a pair of dark green cotton slacks. Changing her clothes, she deposited the key in a deep pocket of the slacks where a smaller pocket was hidden.

Slowing, Lissa caught sight of her pale features in the large mirror over her bureau. A dangling gold ring, hung by a chain around her neck, glinted in the remaining sunlight that slanted across her bedroom. She touched it. Karl had given the ring to her—years ago, when they were children, as a symbol of their friendship. It was a family heirloom.

Lissa's voice was firm in the silence of her room. "Wherever you are, Karl, I'll find you. Just give me half a chance." She added, "Help him be okay, Lord. Please. Protect Karl from whatever he's gotten into."

It did not take long to pick up the order of pizza Cynthia had phoned into the restaurant. The aroma of sausage, tomatoes, and green peppers filled Lissa's car as she wove her way through traffic. Any other time the odor would have been appetizing. Tonight, it made her nauseous.

Lissa signaled and turned right, glancing at the traffic behind her in the rearview mirror. It was dusk. A car, gray and streamlined, pulled in behind her and, at that moment, the driver turned on its lights. Lissa adjusted her mirror against the glare and concentrated on the traffic ahead.

A few minutes later, Lissa signaled for a left turn across traffic, paused to wait for a break, then pulled into the parking lot under the lighted sign heralding Created Images and the studio's entwined L&C logogram. The front office was dark, but Lissa knew the back work rooms would be lit. Another car followed, the headlights causing a momentary flash across her car. Slowing to a stop, Lissa peered over her shoulder and watched as the car swung a circle about the empty lot. It turned to the exit, then merged with evening traffic, returning the way it had come.

The car was gray.

Lissa snagged her lip with her teeth. She tried to ignore the nagging sense of fear that seemed to have descended on her. Steering her car around the building driveway to the back, she turned into her parking spot. Darkness was deepening by the minute. Balancing the two boxes of pizza, Lissa rattled her keys as she struggled from the car. A single bulb lit the back entrance, illuminating a stretched circular patch of light down the solid door and onto the concrete at her feet.

As she located the key she was looking for, she stopped. The rattling of keys silenced. Her hair crawled on the back of her neck.

- 4 -

Lissa looked around with a sharp jerk.

The parking light cast a feeble violet glow over the four parked cars. On the far side of the cars was a concrete block wall, six feet high.

Nerves tense, Lissa listened. She could hear the muted bustle of traffic. Peculiar shadows danced in the obscure light. A chill gust of wind rattled the trees, their branches scraping at each other, stripping themselves of their withered leaves. Showers of leaves skittered and rolled across the top of the cars, onto the pavement.

Lissa's glance flicked to the corners of the lot, to the trees, to the light, searching for something...anything.

Abruptly, she turned back to the door. She inserted her key in the lock and swung the door open, stepping inside quickly to secure it behind her. Her breath came out as a short burst of air.

"There you are!" Cynthia rounded the corner. "About time, too. Donny's threatening to go on strike."

"Not so!" came a disembodied voice from the color lab. "I only offered to scale the wall and go for sandwiches at the deli, that's all."

Lissa moved forward and saw her lab technician's lanky form sprawled in a swivel chair. He pushed away from the work table, dropping proofs and color filters into a pile as he moved. "That smells *good*!" Adolescent greed lit the teenager's eyes as he reached to take the pizza.

"Hi, Lissa," came Julie's soft voice as she emerged from the basement. She carried a load of invoices and an odd assortment of various-sized boxes and envelopes. "It's good to see you back." Her smile accompanied a twinkle in her eyes, and she added, "Now maybe we'll get some organization around here again."

"It hasn't been *that* bad," Cynthia fired in retaliation.

Julie ignored Cynthia and raised knowing brows toward Lissa. "Wait until you see what's lurking in the darkroom." Over her shoulder she added to Donny, "Save me at least two pieces. I'll be right back."

Having already made headway into the first pizza, Donny grunted a reply.

Lissa passed through the doorway of her office and laid her purse on the desk. She saw a stack of messages in the center of the blotter and began shuffling through them.

"Is there anything important I should see first?" Lissa asked Cynthia, who had followed her into the office.

"This," her business partner answered. Cynthia dropped a slice of oozing pizza on a wad of napkins and placed it on Lissa's desk. "I grabbed it before Donny could sink his teeth into it. Better eat fast. He'll be on the prowl for anything left behind."

"I'm not hungry," Lissa replied.

"Since when do airlines feed you such good food that you can turn down fresh pizza?"

"Did Karl leave any other messages?"

Cynthia shrugged her shoulders. "I don't know. Julie took all the calls."

Lissa brushed past Cynthia, headed for the color lab, saying, "Julie, when Karl called, what exactly did he say?"

Julie's dark eyes widened as she hastily swallowed her mouthful of food. "Just that he would try calling later and that he would meet you at the airport."

"No explanation or anything?"

Julie looked puzzled. "About what?"

Lissa waved a hand. "Nothing," she said. "Forget it."

Cynthia followed Lissa back to her office. "You seem a bit disjointed. What's the matter? Didn't Karl meet you at the airport?"

Lissa slid her hands into the pockets of her slacks. The small inner pocket brushed the back of her hand.

Lissa shrugged in answer to Cynthia's questions. "He's a busy man," she said. "I'm certain he'll catch up with me sooner or later. He'd better," she managed a quick smile she hoped masked the worry she knew would be in her eyes, "if he knows what's good for him, anyway."

Cynthia grinned. "I wish that guy would see that *you're* good for him."

"Don't get started," Lissa reprimanded as good-naturedly as she could. "You know Karl doesn't have that in mind. Neither do I. We're good friends. That's all we've ever been. He's like another brother to me. Besides, he's married to his work. You know what he does can be," a spurt of fear shot through her, "dangerous."

"All the more reason for the guy to get out of the business of foreign journalism. I tell you, some of the articles I've read that he's written...and the *pictures*. It gives me the willies just knowing he's been there. It's a wonder he hasn't been shot or kidnapped or something."

"Yes," Lissa replied, the word coming out with a sharpness she could not prevent. She pushed her index finger

23

against the pile of messages and lifted the corners, scattering them in a flutter across her desk.

Cynthia's usually happy features sobered. "Something's bothering you."

"Listen, Cynthia," Lissa grabbed her purse and keys from off the top of her desk, "I've got to go."

"But the color work...and the proofs. Mrs. Barstow's proofs. They're fantastic. You've gotta see them."

"Later. Something's come up."

Cynthia's mouth opened to protest again, but she stopped. Lissa could see the frank puzzlement and worry on her friend's face.

"Okay," Cynthia relented carefully. "Donny and I'll take care of what needs to be done. And I won't have Julie package the proofs until after you've seen them tomorrow. You will be in tomorrow, won't you?"

"Yes, of course I will," Lissa assured her. "I'm sorry. I have something I have to do now."

"It doesn't have anything to do with Karl, does it?"

"I'll explain it all to you later." She smiled suddenly, touching Cynthia's arm. "You're a great friend, you know that?"

"Sure," Cynthia said with a wave of her hand. "You go on. If you find Karl, tell him I said he should quit running all over the world, settle down, and look seriously at you."

"When I see Karl...I'll say nothing of the kind."

Uttering brief good-byes, Lissa made her way back to her car and slammed the door shut against the swirl of chill wind that crept inside with her.

Lissa had no set idea what she should do. She looked around her at the shadowed trees and cars. She could not shake the persistent nagging that prickled the back of her neck.

Inserting the key in the ignition, she turned the car on.

24

The thought of Karl being hurt sent a spasm of anguish through her.

Where was he? Had he gotten medical treatment?

What had Karl entrusted to her?

Father...help me, she prayed as she turned her car into traffic. *I am totally in your hands. Please lead me in the right direction. Help me to know what I'm supposed to do. I'm really afraid for Karl—that he's gotten into more than he can handle. I know he's hurt, Lord. He looked so awful at the airport...and the blood....Please help him be okay. Help us both.*

Lissa fought the worried feeling that threatened to overtake her. She had to trust God to show her what was needed, knowing He would do what was best.

She sighed. Her fingers raked through her hair. There were times that trusting God was difficult.

Returning to her apartment, Lissa mounted the short flight of stairs to her floor and walked down the hall. The hall light glowed in the stillness. It was quiet. Too quiet. Lissa shook away the gnawing uneasiness that fretted her nerves. Until Karl contacted her, other than pray, what could she do?

Taking her keys in one hand and the doorknob in the other, Lissa started to insert the apartment key into the lock.

Her hand jerked away from the doorknob. She stared at the tacky ooze stuck to her fingertips. It was red, very dark.

The apartment door swung open at her touch.

"Karl?"

Lissa walked into the silence of her apartment. Her open patio door could be seen in the low light of the hanging lamp she had left on. The draft caused by opening the front door sent the vertical blinds bowing inward, swinging forward to curl and snap back against the glass with slow, successive cracks.

Lissa moved into the living room. "Karl...are you here?"

The bathroom light shone into the hall. She turned that direction...and stopped to stare at the peculiar, discolored spots on her cream carpet. Hardly daring to, Lissa touched a fingertip to a small dot. Sticky. Dark red. Her hands began to shake. "Karl, if you're here, you're scaring me. Please say something."

The bathroom was empty. Blood stained towels and bandages littered the counter top. Lissa did not stop, but went on to her bedroom. Nothing was disturbed. She whirled and raced back to the living room and passed through the sliders.

"Karl!" Lissa whispered harshly into the darkened bushes beyond the railing. From her level it was a four foot drop to the ground. "Karl, I want to help!"

There was no answer. Only the whisper of the wind.

– 5 –

Lissa made a number of notations on a product order form, then scratched out the last figure with an abrupt movement. Air whistled between her teeth. She adjusted the notation to the correct figure.

Lissa's entire day had been that way...one small mishap after another, with nothing going right. She was nearly late to a commercial shoot that morning. Somehow the color chemicals became contaminated, so the equipment had to be cleaned and the chemicals changed. And now she could not get the simplest supply order straight.

The night before had been a futile attempt at rest. Her nerves trembled with weariness and irritation. She knew she had been short with everyone in the office, including Cynthia who was trying her best to understand what was going on. But how could Lissa explain to Cynthia what was happening when even she did not know?

That in itself was the major problem Lissa had to admit. *She did not know.* She did not know what Karl had done, why he had done it, or how he was now. With the answers to those questions eluding her, and memories of blood on her hands and in her apartment, well, Lissa's nerves were frazzled.

More than once Lissa had considered calling the police. She knew something like this was not a matter she should keep to herself. It was serious, not something she should ignore or try to handle herself. But the sound of Karl's voice stopped her. She would never forgive herself if anything happened to Karl. Neither could she cast off the fervent loyalty she felt toward him and the sense of duty toward what he had asked.

"Excuse me...."

Looking up from her work, Lissa saw Julie peering around the corner of the doorway. "What is it?" Lissa asked.

"We've received a phone call I thought you'd better take. It's a Mrs. Craymore. She's asked that you take family portraits and pictures of their home."

Dropping her pen, Lissa leaned back in her chair. "Can't you make an appointment for her?"

"Tomorrow?"

"Julie, you know we're booked solid for the next six weeks."

"That's what I told her, but she says it's important you come tomorrow."

"I'm afraid that's not possible."

"This is Olivia Craymore...Senator Craymore's wife. She apologized—said she realized you had commitments, but was wondering if there was any possibility you could adjust your scheduling. I think...you should talk to her. She talked about her home being featured in a national magazine and her desire to have you do the work."

Lissa stopped for a moment. With a sigh, she said, "Okay. I'll talk to her."

"She's waiting on line one."

"Bring me the appointment book so I know exactly what

I'm up against if I have to reschedule."

Julie disappeared and Lissa punched the appropriate button on her telephone.

"Mrs. Craymore...this is Lissa McIntyre. What can I do for you?"

"Miss McIntyre, I do appreciate your willingness to talk with me. I realize you must be busy, but I understand you do tremendously wonderful work. My husband, Senator Craymore, mentioned he understood from a colleague that you take lovely portraits."

"Thank you," Lissa murmured. "Typically, however," she nodded as Julie returned with the appointment book, "we make appointments in advance." Lissa scanned the book, turning pages for the next few days to come.

"I understand that. I don't want to be an imposition to you, but we've just been notified that our home has been chosen to be featured in an upcoming magazine presentation, and my husband expressed his desire to have you take the pictures."

"Assignments like those are usually photographed by the magazine's own photographers."

"We've been told we can use someone from our own area—give a local artist coverage. You would, of course, receive full recognition for your work, with each photograph given your byline."

Lissa's pen tapped the page in front of her. There was a possibility...if Cynthia covered the wedding...and they both worked late the next few nights. And Donny had been itching to try his hand with portrait work. "You make it very tempting, Mrs. Craymore. My receptionist said something about tomorrow...?"

Lissa penciled in 2:00 in the afternoon and wrote down the directions to Senator Craymore's home.

As she hung up, Lissa had a smile on her face.

This could prove to be interesting.

– 6 –

Lissa snapped the hatchback on her car and shifted her load of camera equipment. A pair of men were coming down the set of stairs off the open, front patio of Senator Craymore's home. Both men gave automatic smiles as they greeted Lissa and offered to help her with her equipment.

In spite of a second sleepless night filled with worry for Karl, Lissa was looking forward to today's shoot. She had heard stories about Senator Craymore's elaborate home. Her appointment was verified by security at a spot halfway up the meandering drive to the secluded acreage. The senator claimed an inheritance paid for the construction, not taxpayer's money. Of course there were those who disagreed with that assertion, but Lissa knew some people would disbelieve any politician could be as honest and congenial as Senator Craymore's public appearance implied.

The house was a massive assortment of brick, glass, and angles, and for a front door so large, it opened silently, swinging back to reveal a vaulted ceiling two and a half stories high. A stairway curved upward to split at different levels and join opposite balconies for two distinct areas of the house.

As soon as she saw him, Lissa recognized the senator. He was older, distinguished, short of stature, but gave the impression of great confidence in himself. He descended the last few steps of the stairway. His full smile carried over to the firmness of his handshake. Lissa found herself smiling back.

"So glad to have you with us, Miss McIntyre."

"The pleasure is mine," Lissa replied, distinctly aware of her impulse to lower her voice against the reverberating echoes of the senator's voice.

"You come highly recommended."

"I trust my work will be to your satisfaction."

"I've no doubt it will," the senator agreed. He touched his palms together briefly. "My wife will be down soon. Olivia's supervising our daughter's dressing. You did say you would take pictures of the house first, is that right?"

"Certainly, if that is more convenient for you."

"Where would you like to start?"

"I'd like to wander, if you don't mind—to get the feel of the house. If there is anything in particular you would like to have pictures taken of, please let me know."

"My wife would be better at that than I. Talk to me about politics and I can hold my ground. Households..." he gave a short, deep burst of laughter, "I leave that to the true expert."

The senator changed subjects with only a slight pause. "We will have someone with you during your time here." His uplifted hand indicated the two men who had come in with Lissa. After depositing her equipment in a neat pile inside the door, they had taken positions at opposite ends of the foyer. "We have so many antiques, you understand— family heirlooms and the like. There was an unfortunate

31

incident about a year ago when an heirloom of my wife's disappeared during an informal gathering. A distasteful happening. You understand."

"That won't be necessary, Walter," the resonate sound of a male voice drifted over the lower level balcony. "I'd be happy to assist Miss McIntyre's endeavors."

Lissa stared as the man made his way down the curving steps of the stairway.

A pleased smile came to the senator's face. "You know each other?" he asked.

"We are acquaintances," Brent Jamison acknowledged. He came to a stop alongside the senator. "How are you doing this afternoon, Miss McIntyre?"

"Well. Thank you," Lissa managed to answer.

"And your hand?"

"Fine. Really." She resisted the desire to shove her hand in her pocket. "It was nothing."

"An injury of some form?" the senator asked.

"Nothing serious," Lissa heard herself say past the pounding of her heart. "Mr. Jamison assisted me at the airport day before yesterday."

"Due to your distinguished company, then," the senator's smile took in both Lissa and Brent Jamison, "I feel free to allow you full rein in our household."

Lissa found herself murmuring an appreciative comment to the senator's remark.

"If you don't mind," the senator's hands came together to produce a dry, rasping sound, "I will check my wife's progress. Brent," the senator addressed the man next to him. Brent's unusual, sober gaze lingered on Lissa, then turned to Walter Craymore. "We'll continue our discussion later. You will stay for dinner, won't you?"

"I may have other plans. We'll see, Senator."

The two security men disappeared. Lissa unpacked her camera under the watchful eye of Brent Jamison. Whoever

32

he was, he was trusted within the Craymore household.

She worked to cover her nervousness. Her equipment took little time to ready. Striding across the floor, Lissa searched for the best angle to capture the look of the massive entry. She focused and took a picture.

"No flash?"

Lissa glanced briefly at Mr. Jamison. "I like to work with natural lighting whenever possible."

"You have quite a flair for it, too. How would I know?" he asked at the look she sent his way. "You did quite well in the photo essay contest 'A Day in the Life of Iowa'."

Lissa walked through an archway into a lovely drawing room. *How did he know that?* A baby grand piano monopolized a corner near a set of French doors. Outside the doors, Lissa could see a secluded nook filled with the glow of the afternoon sun.

"Are you a photo enthusiast, Mr. Jamison?" She hoped the question was casual enough.

"As I recall—you took first place in the People Profile division and did the cover photo for the book the sponsors published."

"I'm pleased you remember my work."

What might possibly pass for a grin momentarily touched the corners of Mr. Jamison's dry mouth. "I remembered your partner's work—her photo of a photographer photographing an outdoor wedding. Your picture of the bride on the terrace was elegant, but I much preferred your partner's shot capturing your spontaneous encouragement to the bride. 'Smile'," he pantomimed, eyes lighting as his hand lifted in imitation of her pose. His hand dropped to touch the curve of the piano. "I knew I'd seen you somewhere before we met at the airport."

"Should I be flattered you remember my picture?"

His fingers tripped down an octave of keys. The blend of

sounds lingered. "You're a very beautiful woman, Miss McIntyre."

Lissa's cheeks warmed under his sober scrutiny. "Excuse me, Mr. Jamison," she said, indicating that he move out of her shot.

"Brent," he said, not moving.

Lissa stopped, lowering her camera. Her gaze took him in. Lissa drew a slow breath. "Brent," she complied. "Satisfied?" Lissa tempered the last word with a slight lifting of her lips.

An eyebrow rose, along with one corner of his mouth. Brent moved over to the side. Lissa framed her shot, taking advantage of the sheer-softened glow from the doors. She tripped the shutter.

"Then it was you," Lissa said, "who recommended my work to Senator Craymore."

"Do you mind? I know you do good work, so I haven't led Walter astray."

"I appreciate the business and the opportunity to have my pictures in a national magazine."

"Enough to have dinner with me tonight?"

Lissa waited several seconds as she digested the question and adjusted the setting on her camera. "I thought you were expected to have dinner with Senator Craymore."

"I told him I might be busy. How adventuresome are you?"

Their footsteps tapped polished hardwood floors. "What has adventure got to do with it?"

"Is that your form of self-defense?"

Lissa stopped and looked at the man who turned in front of her. "What are you talking about?"

"Answering my question with a question."

"I don't know you, Mr. Jamison. My family taught me to be careful with strangers."

"I won't be a stranger if you have dinner with me."

34

"I don't think I like you very much, Mr. Jamison."

"Brent," he said. "No, I suppose not. I'm told I have an abrasive attitude and am not very tactful."

"And you're in politics?"

"Whatever gave you that idea?"

Lissa shrugged. Her gaze swept the view of the library they had come to, then returned to the man. "Association," she replied. "My mistake."

"Justifiable. My father and Walter go back many years. They attended college together, in fact. My father went into business, Walter into politics. Walter and I are friendly," he paused, "associates."

"And your father?"

Brent's hands slid into the pockets of his slacks. "Dead. Five years ago."

"I'm sorry," she said, her voice subdued.

"Don't be. He'd been sick for a long time." His shoulders flexed as if to shrug off memories, then, "Dinner?...In spite of the fact that you've decided you don't like me very much?"

"Tonight?" Lissa strode across the room and up a flight of open stairs to look back to a grouping of casually elegant furniture arranged for comfortable reading.

"Are you busy?" Brent asked from below.

"I'll be catching up on backlogged darkroom work. My partner is a wizard with cameras, but slow in the darkroom."

Brent stepped out of camera range. Lissa clicked off the shot, then changed the angle and took another.

"You're going to have to eat sometime," he said.

"Are we back to dinner again?"

"I'm also known to be persistent."

Lissa came back down the stairs. "Sorry. I am busy."

"I'll pick you up at 8:00. Will that give you enough time to do your work?"

"I had planned to stay the entire evening." They entered

an expansive dining hall. Crystal chandeliers hung above the longest table Lissa had ever seen. She reached into her bag to pull out a star filter and attach it to the front of her lens.

"You wouldn't want people to accuse you of overworking yourself, would you?" Brent's voice came from the side.

The short sound Lissa made could not quite be classified as laughter. "As long as I have the proofs out on time, people don't care whether I overwork myself. Besides," she said, meeting his gaze, "I like what I do. Very much."

"A couple hours off shouldn't matter."

"I've been away on vacation. I need to catch up on my work."

"Pretend it's an extension of your vacation. Nine o'clock?" he asked.

The man *was* persistent. She had to give him credit for that. Lissa walked from one side of the room to the other. She wanted to capture the effect of the chandeliers in just the right light.

"Have you ever had Greek food?" Brent asked.

Lissa answered, "I can't say that I have." She tripped the shutter.

"You're in for a treat. I know an excellent place. It's new and the food is great."

Lissa lowered her camera with a sigh. "Mr. Jamison..."

"Brent," he said. "Give it up and say, 'Yes'."

Lissa looked at the man who walked toward her and stopped just a few feet away. His blue-flecked brown eyes watched her. Something about his stance, the way he saw her, caught her attention.

"Yes," Lissa said, then wondered, *Now why did I say that?*

– 7 –

"Maryanne, don't wiggle so much," Olivia Craymore admonished her daughter quietly.

"But, Mommy, this dress is itchy, and I want to go play with Dallas."

Lissa stepped back with the camera release in her hand and raised a finger to the senator and his wife. She smiled. They smiled. Lissa asked Maryanne, "Who's Dallas?"

An animated gleam filled the young girl's face. Lissa snapped the picture.

"He's my puppy," Maryanne exclaimed. "He came from one of Daddy's friends in Texas. He's my very best friend."

Lissa quickly adjusted their seating arrangement, helping Maryanne to sit across her father's knee. She folded Maryanne's hands and rested them on the little girl's lap, holding them there briefly as she said, "You'll have to introduce me to Dallas when we're all done." Lissa stepped back, continuing to smile, and caught the senator and his wife's attention. "Do you think Dallas will like me?"

Maryanne laughed. The shutter clicked. "Dallas loves anyone who will scratch his ears," the little girl declared.

"Then I'll be sure to scratch his ears," Lissa said, adding, "I once had a dog named Colorado."

"Was he a Irish Setter like Dallas?"

"He was part Collie, and my brothers and I sure loved him a lot. Smile," Lissa said. She snapped off another shot. "We're done. Now that wasn't so bad, was it?"

"I'll get Dallas!" Maryanne exclaimed as she scrambled off her father's lap. The senator chuckled at his daughter's enthusiasm. Somewhere in the house a telephone rang.

"You certainly have a way with children, Miss McIntyre," Olivia Craymore said. "I thought we'd never get a decent shot of Maryanne. She's such a busy child."

Lissa began to gather her equipment. "I like the challenge of children, Mrs. Craymore. Maryanne is a delight and her enthusiasm will be wonderful on film. You'll see when I bring the proofs back in a couple weeks." Lissa slid her camera into its case and began to retract the tripod.

Looking askance at the highly polished flooring, Olivia said, "Perhaps we should go outside so Dallas won't scar the floor. I'm afraid Dallas is as enthusiastic about life as Maryanne—and we've had one incident already today."

"Senator..." a man interrupted quietly from the doorway of the drawing room.

"Of course," the senator nodded. He turned toward Lissa. "Miss McIntyre," he took her hand in a final, generous clasp. "I'm certain we will be more than pleased with the results of your work. But if you will excuse me, I believe there is a phone call I've been waiting for."

Lissa murmured her understanding and barely had time to return her attention to Olivia when a bounding streak of red fur burst into the room.

"Maryanne!" Olivia exclaimed. She sighed, but lovingly.

"Isn't he beautiful, Miss Lissa? I just love him." Maryanne dropped to her knees to hug her half-grown puppy around the neck. Dallas quivered with energy.

"He's lovely," Lissa agreed, squatting to Maryanne's level. She scratched Dallas behind the ears. "You know what, though? I think maybe we should take Dallas outside so I can see him run. What do you think?"

Maryanne's eyes widened soberly. "We had an accident this morning." Her voice lowered. "One of Mommy's favorite bowls."

Lissa's tone imitated Maryanne's. "Then we'd better see that Dallas isn't where he shouldn't be. He's still a baby and doesn't know any better, yet."

With Lissa and Olivia following, Maryanne took a firm grip on Dallas's collar, leading the way through a number of rooms to a set of French doors opening onto the backyard. Successive tiers of brick patio fanned downward in the direction of the pool and garden area Lissa had photographed earlier. Fall had painted its colors in the trees, but it was warmer today than yesterday and peacefully quiet...until Dallas, barking, streaked across the yard in pursuit of a squirrel. Maryanne raced after her puppy.

Lissa and Olivia stood together taking in the view. The air was crisp. The puppy yapped. Maryanne twirled in circles with Dallas, her laughter floating back across the yard.

"You have a lovely family and home," Lissa said. "It's been a privilege being asked to photograph both."

Olivia remained silent for a space of time as she watched her daughter play. A slow smile graced the corners of her beautiful mouth. "There are times...it's worth it all." After a brief pause, she said, "I understand Brent kept you company earlier. I didn't know the two of you knew each other."

"We don't. Not really. We met recently at the airport."

A fleeting frown touched Olivia's face. "Brent was at the airport?"

"He helped me to my car."

"I see." There was silence that stretched to a long minute. "If you will excuse me," Olivia said suddenly, "I have some things that require my attention. If you have trouble finding your way back, please ask Franklin," she indicated a man standing discretely to one side, out of hearing. "He will be happy to assist you." Olivia Craymore turned quickly, her heels tapping on the brick paving. Lissa watched her go, wondering what she had said to produce Olivia's reaction.

"Miss Lissa! Come down!" Maryanne waved, catching Lissa's attention. "See how Dallas catches his ball." Lissa hesitated, looking once more in the direction Olivia Craymore had disappeared. *"Miss Lissa!"*

"I'm coming," Lissa said and hurried down the patio levels to a wide carpet of green grass. The time of year had yet to catch up with the Craymore's lawn.

"Watch," Maryanne said and threw the ball into the air. Dallas leaped, caught it, and raced around his mistress, refusing to release the ball. Lissa watched as Maryanne ran off after her puppy.

Far off across the lawn a man stood in the shadow of a tree that bordered the oasis of green surrounding the Craymore home. To her right, Franklin remained in close proximity. Lissa realized her every movement was being observed. She turned to look back toward the house. The late afternoon sun created shadows in various recesses. She spied another man off the terrace. Strange that so many people would be needed for security...but then Lissa remembered reports of an attempt on the senator's life ten months earlier. Doubtless that was a factor.

Lissa took in the obvious signs of wealth about her and saw not three, but four men, out of close range, but definitely not out of sight.

How could the Craymores be comfortable living in this

kind of atmosphere? With every movement observed by other people?

As Lissa watched the house, the senator came out a door, talking with a taller man. She watched until the two men disappeared into one of the alcoves surrounding the house.

Where had Brent gone when she started taking the family portraits?

Lissa looked at her watch.

Maryanne returned, breathless, but in possession of the ball. "I really must go," Lissa said. "Thank you for sharing Dallas with me. He's a beautiful dog."

"Will you be back?" Maryanne asked.

"In a couple of weeks. You'll be able to see your pictures then."

Lissa left Maryanne with Dallas when the little girl said she'd rather stay with her puppy, and retraced her steps back through the Craymore house. Although not directly in her footsteps, it was obvious she was being followed.

Truth be known, Lissa would be grateful to be gone. Having her every movement watched was slightly disconcerting. Besides, there *was* a lot of work to catch up on at the studio.

Coming to the room where she had left her equipment, Lissa found her cameras gone. A servant passing through informed her that her equipment had been left ready at the front door. Making her way to the entry, Lissa found her things dismantled and packed and placed together in an orderly fashion. Another servant waited nearby to help Lissa carry them to the car.

As she began to gather her things, Brent appeared from a side room. Lissa said, "I thought you had left."

"I was waiting for you." Brent picked up a case, dismissing the servant. "I was hoping I might be able to persuade you to go sooner than 9:00." He opened the door and indicated that Lissa go ahead of him. "Nine won't leave

41

time for a leisurely meal or much conversation."

"You implied you would be satisfied however late the hour," she could not resist saying.

"If that's all I can have. But, seriously…what do you say? Let's make it 8:00."

Lissa located the key to her car and popped the hatchback open. "I might be able to make it by 8:00. It all depends on what Cynthia's been able to accomplish this afternoon."

"Maybe she's done it all," came Brent's reply. His mouth was not as tight as she remembered it. It was almost soft, expressive. "Then we could leave at 7:00."

Lissa looked up at the man beside her. She wondered if he ever truly smiled. "I'll see what I can do," she said.

- 8 -

Cynthia had accomplished far more than Lissa had hoped. Lissa adjusted the easel by feel and touched the timer. A negative exposure of a group of 5 x 7 portraits shimmered in the darkroom. The timer shut down automatically, leaving Lissa in the dark. She closed the easel cover, then adjusted the lens above it to permit a page of billfold photographs to be exposed next. With the completion of this order...she checked over her shoulder to see the luminous dial of a small clock...she could be out of Creative Images and home in plenty of time before Brent arrived.

Even as the thought came to mind, Lissa could only wonder how she had allowed herself to be talked into going out to dinner with Brent Jamison...especially with Karl out there, somewhere...who knew where?

It was frightening, not knowing just how badly hurt he might be...or what Karl, in reality, expected of her. Lissa prayed that, despite indications otherwise, Karl was not seriously hurt.

43

Her stomach rumbled. Lissa's lips tightened. She had skipped lunch.

Which brought her mind back to dinner and Brent Jamison. What did she know about the man? Come to think of it—she frowned—he never did tell her what he did for a living...except to give the impression he was not in politics. As she reached to trip the timer, Lissa realized she didn't even know that for certain.

Her sigh was loud in the confined quarters.

Lord...why am I doing this? Karl is...well, he's out there somewhere injured, hurting, maybe worse...and I'm...going out on a date? Her head shook again as the glow in front of her faded away.

"You're crazy, Lissa," she muttered. "But what can you do? Karl says, 'Play Resistance,' so I play Resistance. Life is routine—nothing out of the ordinary. But, Lord," her thoughts redirected themselves, "something's got to give somewhere. I feel odd going with this man. I should be looking for Karl, doing something constructive—not having dinner at some Greek restaurant. I don't even know what Greek food *looks* like, let alone tastes like," she sighed and said to herself, "...as if that has any bearing on the situation."

A scratchy fingernail tap swept across the outside of the darkroom door. "Quit muttering in there," came Cynthia's voice.

"I'm almost done," Lissa said, detaching the exposed photographic paper from the end of the roll. She slipped it into a light-proof container and pushed the light switch on. So much for that. The rest was up to Cynthia tonight. She was through, and she said so when she came out the door and handed the exposed material to Cynthia.

"Just run it once and leave the test prints for Donny to check color exposure tomorrow," Lissa said.

"But where are you going?" Cynthia asked. "I thought we were going to finish these orders. It was your idea, remember?"

"I'm sorry, Cynthia, but something's come up."

"Again?" came the perplexed tone. "You know I've barely seen you in this office all day today. Not that I expected you here, but you said we'd get this work done tonight." Suddenly her face lifted, brightening with realization. "Karl!" An adoring groan came from Cynthia as she hugged the tube of paper to her chest. "Break my heart," she said. "Get out of here. I forgive you. Grab that man whenever—"

"It's not Karl!" Lissa insisted, then felt instantly guilty at the look that transformed Cynthia's face. Lissa paced across the color lab while her hand lifted with an abrupt movement. "I'm sorry. It's been an...unusual day."

Cynthia placed the tube on a table and followed Lissa across the room. "What's wrong? This is Cynthia, remember—spacey and annoying at times, but still your friend." Cynthia hesitated. "You haven't seemed yourself since you got home from Colorado." She touched Lissa's arm. "Is there something I can do to help?"

Lissa drew a couple deep breaths. Stomach churning with indecision, her hands suddenly cartwheeled in the air. "This whole thing is crazy," she said. "I'm not supposed to talk to anyone." Perplexed confusion crossed Cynthia's face. "I'm supposed to be playing a game...only there is something very wrong about this game."

"What are you talking about?"

"'Resistance.' It's a game we played as children—Karl and I and my brothers. Two days ago at the airport Karl asked me to play Resistance. He warned me not to trust anyone and gave me a key. For what, I don't know, and don't ask me from whom," she said even as Cynthia began to form the words. "I have no idea. He didn't tell me. And then, after he left, I discovered the key was coated with blood—fresh blood...Karl's. And I'm not talking about your cut finger type variety of blood."

Cynthia's eyes grew.

45

"Karl is hurt," Lissa said. "Badly...I know it. He looked terrible at the airport—"

"Then you did see him!"

Lissa nodded, adding, "When I got home after being here that night he'd been at my apartment, too. Cynthia," Lissa looked sick, "there were drops of blood on my carpet...and in my bathroom."

"Have you heard from him since?"

Defeated, Lissa shook her head. "I can't imagine where he might be. He said he couldn't go to his apartment, and he had no place else to go. He wasn't in any position to travel...and," the last phrase came out with disgust, "I'm going out on a date tonight!"

Aghast, Cynthia accused, "How can you be thinking about dates at a time like this?"

"I'm not! It's just...I didn't...." Lissa's hands flew through the air. "I was conned!...And I'm certain I couldn't get out of it if I tried."

"You've got to find Karl. Call this guy—this date of yours—and cancel. Better yet, who is he? I'll call and tell him you're sick."

"You can't lie like that."

Cynthia straightened her stance. "Then I'll tell him you have business that absolutely has to be taken care of."

"You don't know Brent Jamison. He doesn't take 'no' for an answer."

"Who is this Brent Jamison? I've never heard you talk about him before."

"That's just the point," Lissa said. "I really don't know the man. I met him the first time at the airport, then again today at Senator Craymore's home."

"How odd....You actually accepted a date with a man you don't know?"

"The man's very persuasive."

"Is he in politics?"

"I don't know," Lissa said. "I don't know what that's got to do with it, anyway."

"Well, I'm calling the guy," Cynthia said as she made her way to her office. "First things first. We're going to get you out of this predicament. As for Karl..." her look became disturbed as she leafed through the telephone book, "Lissa...what can Karl be doing?"

"That's the very question I've been asking myself repeatedly the past 48 hours."

Cynthia found the name and punched out a series of numbers as the two women exchanged troubled looks.

Mimicking Julie's most professional tone, Cynthia exchanged greetings with someone on the other end. Lissa wondered if Brent would listen to Cynthia but got the impression from the conversation that Brent was not home. Cynthia left a message canceling Lissa's obligation and hung up.

"Who was it?" Lissa asked.

"A woman. She sounded older. Now what do we do?"

"It's not what *we* do, but me. I can't involve you any further than I already have."

"What are you *talking* about?" Cynthia squeaked. "I am involved already. There is *no way* you are keeping me out of this."

"At this point, the best way you can help is to pray...and let me know if Karl calls. If he does, get some information out of him." A thought came to mind. "I think I'll try going to his apartment. He left a message on my answering machine saying he couldn't go there, but that doesn't mean I can't. Somewhere we've got to find a clue...something to help us out."

Cynthia's eyes widened suddenly. "Have you picked up his mail this week?"

Lissa stared at Cynthia. "I would think he would have...." Her mind spun with possibilities. "We don't know for sure,

47

do we? If he didn't have time to do that...it's a perfect excuse for going, isn't it?"

Hands on hips, Cynthia demanded, "What are you waiting for?"

Since Karl was gone so much of the time, he had his mail delivered to a box at the main post office. Lissa's weekly habit whenever Karl was out of town was to pick up his mail and take it to his apartment. Having been in Colorado at Jake's wedding for the last week, she had neglected to do that task...and so had Karl, she discovered.

Lissa scanned the pieces of mail, half hoping to find something, anything that would help her.

She was disappointed. There was nothing.

The drive from the post office to Karl's west side apartment took less than twenty minutes. Lissa wheeled into the first available parking slot she came to in front of Karl's apartment building. She grabbed the stack of mail and heaved a short, worried sigh. Her stomach became slightly queasy.

The brick building was bathed in the glow of yard lights. A chill breeze tugged at Lissa's clothes. She hurried through the front door into the foyer, nearly running into a young man—the apartment manager—who was collecting his mail and paper.

"Hey, Lissa," Jeremy said. "Did the police finally find you? They've been up at Karl's apartment for over an hour."

"Police?" she breathed. "Here?"

"I gave them your number when nobody could figure out where Karl was. Did he leave town again already?" Wrapping his newspaper around a handful of mail, Jeremy didn't wait for an answer. "Seems somebody forced their way in and tore the place up pretty good. Hey, are you okay?" he asked. "I didn't mean to spring it on you like that. I thought you knew what was going on."

"No...no, I didn't. I just brought the mail over." She was beginning to feel sick.

"Karl hasn't picked it up? He's been home a couple days. I've seen him. He didn't tell you he was back?"

"I've...been out of town. My brother got married."

"Congratulations. Come on, I'll walk you up. The police have been questioning everyone, and I know they've been looking for you. They won't let anyone in Karl's place, not even me. You'd think they were dealing with international criminals or something. From what I can tell, they're dusting every square inch of the place."

Jeremy hooked his hand around Lissa's arm and started up a short flight of stairs to a landing. They turned to move up the next flight. Lissa numbly kept pace, her thoughts spinning as her mind worked to make some sense of what she ought to do. She felt lightheaded.

Voices floated down from the upper level. A young woman dashed past them, rolling her eyes at Jeremy at the inconvenience of it all.

Jeremy asked the vanishing figure, "Did they finally finish questioning you, Andrea?"

"Yeah," her voice drifted back. "What could I say? I wasn't even here."

Jeremy shrugged at Lissa's look. "They've questioned all of us pretty extensively. I get the impression this wasn't a simple robbery attempt."

Lissa stopped and gulped, turning to press her back against the wall. Stars spun in her head as visions of her blood-stained fingers replayed themselves in her mind. "Just a minute," she breathed. "I need to..." she sank to the step, "sit down." The last two words became a whisper as she hung her head between her knees.

Lissa heard voices past the roaring in her head. Jeremy was talking and another person answered. She vaguely felt someone touch her neck and draw her hair back. There were questions, but she did not answer as she fought against the darkness that hovered across her mind. Her hands shook.

49

She had never fainted before.

When someone took Karl's mail, she let go willingly. She was told to breathe deeply. Lissa followed directions, frowning as she heard the same person asking if she felt better.

"A little," Lissa answered.

"Can you sit up?"

Lissa drew a couple more breaths.

"Stay there as long as you need to," the man said. His fingertips circled gently between her shoulder blades.

Lissa heard Jeremy say, "Here's a glass of water."

After taking a sip, the sick feeling persisted, but it wasn't as bad as before. Lissa breathed in deeply. Wearily, she lifted her head...and focused on the unusual eyes of Brent Jamison.

– 9 –

Brent stared back at Lissa, his gaze unreadable, but not unconcerned.

Frowning, Lissa asked, "What are you doing here?" She touched her fingertips to her mouth. Cold.

"I happened to be in the neighborhood. Are you feeling better?"

"I...think so. Thank you," she said when Jeremy offered her the glass of water again. Jeremy looked almost as pale as she felt.

The water was cool and helped bring her senses nearer to normal. Lissa tipped her head back against the wall. She closed her eyes, feeling the water travel down her throat. With what strength she regained, she was able to balance the glass on her knee.

Faint voices drifted down the stairwell...and Brent's jacket whispered against itself as he took hold of the limp hand dangling across her other knee. His hands were warm and dry...a far cry from the condition of her own.

Lissa opened her eyes to see Brent watching her.

"Better now?" he asked.

From the position Brent had taken, crouched on the step beside her, Lissa saw where his jacket gaped open. Inside, mostly hidden, was the shadow of a shoulder holster. Her line of vision flicked from the gun to Brent's face. "What are you?"

"I'm a police detective."

Lissa glanced at Jeremy who remained silent. There was a quiet moment as she digested that information.

"I feel awful," she muttered finally.

"Faint?" Brent asked.

She nodded.

"It'll pass," he said.

"I should have eaten lunch."

"Lack of food," he declared. "We should have gone to dinner earlier."

"I cancelled."

"I know. I got the message. I planned to drop by anyway—just in case. As it is, I'll still feed you, but dinner won't be as I planned."

Brent handed Karl's mail and the glass to Jeremy when Lissa explained who the mail belonged to and asked, "Would you go to Mr. Karello's apartment and give these to Detective Hamilton? Tell him Miss McIntyre arrived. I'm taking her across the street to the diner." Jeremy nodded. "Think you can stand now?" Brent asked as Jeremy started up the stairs.

Lissa nodded. She was still queasy as they walked across the street.

The small diner was cramped, with barely sufficient lighting. Lissa slid across the cracked red leather seat of the booth and looked up as their waitress came and placed two glasses of iced water on the table.

The waitress smiled, "What can I get you tonight?"

52

"First, I'd like some coffee," Brent replied. He glanced at Lissa. "Coffee?"

"Hot tea, please." Her hand rubbed her midsection where the nausea persisted—whether from nervousness, lack of food, or both she was not certain, but suspected it was a combination of all that had happened. Lissa let loose a short breath of air. "Could I have some crackers, too?"

"Right away on those crackers," Brent said, handing the pair of menus back to the waitress. "We'll also take two orders of your special. Make them medium rare."

The waitress smiled, her pleasant expression taking them both in.

When the woman left, Brent asked, "How long have you known Karl Karello?"

"Since we were children," Lissa said. "We grew up together, on neighboring farms."

"Do you realize what's going on?"

"What do you mean?"

"You knew Mr. Karello's apartment had been broken into?"

"Jeremy told me," Lissa said.

"Then he didn't summon you?"

"I brought Karl's mail over. I do that every week."

"Do you know where we can locate Mr. Karello?"

"I don't," she said. "I wish I did. Was the break-in...a robbery?"

Brent shrugged, a minute movement that indicated a negative rather than indecision. "Not robbery. The stereo's there, plus a TV, computer," his head tipped, "some money. No...whoever was there was looking for something specific. You wouldn't happen to know what that is, would you?"

Lissa's thoughts turned round in her mind. "Why should I know?" she asked.

"We understand Mr. Karello travels internationally. With all his traveling it might be easy for him to pick up a dangerous sideline to his journalistic endeavors. You wouldn't know if he's involved in anything illegal, would you?"

Lissa's jaw tightened. "Karl isn't a criminal, if that's what you're implying. He's not that type of person. Why don't you ask him all the questions when he comes home?"

"Because," Brent's look drilled through her, "we are concerned Karl may not be able to make it back on his own."

"What...do you mean?"

"The evidence left in his bathroom indicates Karl is suffering from a severe injury."

Her pulse raced. Reluctantly, noting Brent's look, she asked, "Such as...."

"Initial findings lead us to believe it's a gunshot wound...and not one we might simply consider a flesh wound."

Lissa knew whatever color she might have regained was lost. Her hands covered her mouth.

"We need to find Karl, Lissa. We know he hasn't gone to a hospital. If Karl is still alive—"

"*If?*"

"I don't think it's fair for me to try to minimize the seriousness of this situation. We're hoping he is, but..." his voice trailed off. The look on his face was all Lissa had to see to know Brent did not believe Karl could possibly be alive.

"You're wrong. I *know* Karl is still alive."

"How?" The one word came out with sharp emphasis. Brent's look speared her.

Resistance.

Now?

Lissa stared nervously. "I'd know *here*," she stressed, pressing trembling fingers to the rapid pounding that intensified in her chest. Her mind spun. Karl was alive. She

54

had seen him, spoken with him. He had given her...a key.

Concealing evidence.

The man across from her was a detective.

Lissa's thoughts whirled with the uncertainty of her situation.

How much should she divulge?

What was she thinking? Brent is the *police.*

Karl had said to trust no one...but...Lissa chanced a look at Brent...Karl didn't mean...the police, too....Did he?

Silence stretched between them. Lissa's hand pressed against her midsection. Her stomach roiled with a combination of emptiness and fear. Fear for Karl...fear of discovery...fear of doing the wrong thing.

What was she going to do?

Dear Father, I need your help!

"But I don't know what you hope to accomplish here."

"What I hope to accomplish is to learn enough about Karl to answer some of our questions regarding him—why someone would ransack his apartment, and the reason, if he is still alive, why he hasn't seen a doctor or gone to a hospital."

"How do you know he hasn't?"

"The medical profession is required by law to report any gunshot wound," Brent said. "We've already checked with all the hospitals within the state. A man as badly wounded as Karl Karello can't have gone far."

"*If* he's still alive." The slight bitterness that came out was tempered with the dread that Karl could be dying.

Brent stared back at Lissa.

The waitress returned with their drinks and the crackers. Lissa took time to open her tea bag and drop it into her cup of hot water. Her hands shook. She could hear the scrape, scrape of Brent's spoon idly stirring ice into his coffee.

"Tell me about Karl Karello," Brent said.

Lissa looked up into eyes more gray than blue. "Other

than what I've already told you, what do you want to know?"

"Assuming he is running from someone who is trying to kill him—that the gunshot wound was not an accident and that he did not intentionally tear his own apartment apart—is there anyplace he could have gone?" His fingertip touched the table between them. "Someplace he would have felt safe, that a stranger or a person who might not know him intimately would not know about? Does he have relatives? Other close friends he might try to contact?"

Lissa's head shook. "His family is gone. His job keeps him from making close friends."

"You mentioned a farm."

"It's still his," she admitted. "It's southeast of here. But it's rented out—the house, the land. He only has his apartment."

Lissa dropped her tea bag on her spoon, twisted the string around it, and squeezed excess tea from the bag before laying it on her saucer. The spoon rattled against the stoneware. She reached for a packet of crackers from the basket.

Brent's hand snaked out to clutch hers. Lissa gasped, wide-eyed at the glare that suddenly flashed from the detective's darkened eyes.

"Where's the key, Lissa?"

– 10 –

"*What?*" Lissa, shocked, could only stare.

"The key you dropped at the airport. Where is it?"

"It's....What difference does it make?"

Brent twisted Lissa's hand upright to emphasize his words. "You have no cut on your hand," the detective said.

Lissa's expression sagged. He knew.

"If I have the lab test the traces on my handkerchief," his eyes darkened, "it will match what's in the bathroom at Karl Karello's apartment, won't it?"

Lissa numbly watched the man across from her.

"You could have been honest with me," Brent said.

"I have been," she cried, jerking her hand away from him. "I *don't* know where Karl is. That's the truth!"

"Where's the key?"

Her look shifted. "I promised I would keep it for him. He's scared and I know he's hurt. He gave me the key because he didn't know what else to do with it."

"Then you have seen him."

"Yes. No." Lissa made a small sound of frustration. "Not really. He left the key where I could pick it up."

"You realize, of course, that this key is probably the reason he got shot...and why his apartment was ransacked."

"Yes."

"And I could have you arrested for concealing evidence."

Lissa's heart stopped. "Would you?"

Brent sat back in his seat. A look of exasperation and conflict mingled plainly on his face.

Lissa bore his scrutiny, her heart thudding. If he did arrest her, would she give him the key?

What was she *thinking*?

Lord, I'm so confused. Please give me wisdom to know what to do.

"Did he tell you what the key was for?" Brent asked.

"No."

"You have no idea what he's into?"

"Karl's been gone for two months. I came back to town just minutes before you saw me at the airport. I've been back—what? A little over 48 hours? Whatever happened must have occurred within the last 72 hours."

Brent scrutinized her. "How do you know?"

"Karl left messages on my answering machine and at my business."

"What sort of messages?"

"Personal. At least the first two messages were."

"Then?"

"Another message was left shortly after I'd received the key at the airport."

Brent waited for her to continue.

"All Karl said was not to trust anyone. He stressed it so much. Now you see why—"

"But I'm the *police*," Brent's fingertips connected with his chest. "I'm supposed to *help* people in trouble."

"I realize that! Don't you think I've been struggling with

that very thought? I've *never* been in trouble with the police before. I've never even had a speeding ticket! It's just that Karl was adamant. I'm scared," Lissa admitted. "I don't want Karl to die." Her hands brushed her face as her words slowed. "I'm frightened of doing the wrong thing. There was a reason for Karl's warning. I know it. I *know him*. We are Christians." Her chin came up as her gaze met Brent's. "Both of us know God's Son, Jesus Christ, as our Savior. We live by a certain moral standard. That's not to say we're perfect and aren't tempted to do something we know we shouldn't, but illegal practices are not a part of Karl's life. He may be headstrong, but he does not deliberately break the law. If he stressed that I'm not to trust anyone, then," she paused momentarily, taking in Brent's expression, "I don't know...if that...means you, too."

Brent's lips thinned to a fine line as Lissa spoke her last words. She saw the sharp angles of his face, the tight mouth, the look in his eyes. His gaze dropped. Somewhere in the kitchen a rattle of dishes and voices could be heard.

A sigh escaped the detectives's lips. Brent said, "Sometimes I need to be shoved back to reality. I forget there are decent people who are simply frightened by their circumstances—that not everyone is a felon ready to make an illegal fast buck." There was another sigh. "You see, Lissa," Brent went on, "I'm a Christian, too." Lissa's mouth dropped open. "And I know what you are saying about your life." His line of vision came up to connect with hers. "I understand what you said about Karl and yourself." The skin around his eyes appeared to tighten, "But that doesn't solve the problem we still have."

Detective Brent Jamison...a Christian? Lissa managed to retrieve her jaw from its slack position.

"The key..." Brent asked, "is it safe?"

"Yes."

"You still say you don't know what it's for?"

"Karl didn't explain anything to me."

Brent's head nodded once, briefly. He was silent a few moments, his face a study of intensity. "Keep it." Lissa's mouth dropped open again. "No one else knows you have the key?"

"My business partner."

"Will she say anything?"

Lissa managed to shake her head.

"We'll have to confirm that." Then, "Let's wait and see if Karl attempts to reach you. If he does, hopefully, he will give you some clue as to where he's at, what the key is for, and why he's running. If he's not involved in anything illegal, he must not be thinking clearly. If he thinks the police have it, he might run again before we can help him."

"You're using me for bait," Lissa managed to say.

A breath of air sifted through Brent's teeth. "Yeah," he replied grimly, "I am."

"What if the people who are after Karl come after me?"

"I'll be there."

She just looked at him. "You're going to protect me?"

His glance flicked over her face. "Do you object?"

"I don't know. I don't know what to think."

The waitress stopped with their meal. There was a moment of silence until the woman was gone.

"What else are you not telling me?" Brent asked. He dropped a pat of butter in the opened slit of his baked potato. "Do you have any other untold secrets lurking in the shadows? I want to know everything, whether you think it's worth mentioning or not."

Lissa searched the thoughts that came to mind. "The night I came home I went to the office for awhile. When I got back to my apartment, Karl had been there."

"How do you know that?"

Lissa explained.

"He didn't leave anything else behind? No one hanging

around? No other happenings that have you wondering?"

Lissa shook her head with each question.

"When you finish your dinner," Brent said, lifting the tip of his steak knife, "I'll take you home. I'd like to take a look around and see if I can find anything you might have missed."

Lissa looked at the untouched food before her. Her hands pressed against her midsection where her uncertainty and fears were expressing themselves in physical form. "I–I c–can't eat."

Brent's dour expression altered. He reached for the packet of crackers Lissa had been going to pick up. Tearing back the cellophane, he presented them to her. "This will get you started," he said. "The steak is excellent. You need some food."

Looking at Brent for a moment, Lissa slowly accepted the offering. Brent settled back in his seat. Lissa scattered a fine shower of cracker crumbs on the table.

After taking a couple bites in silence, Brent said, "Tell me about yourself."

Lissa's greenish-gray gaze came in contact with his. "Why?"

"I asked before if that was your form of self-protection."

Lissa looked blank.

"At the airport you mentioned five brothers. Did they constantly badger you? Is that the reason you counter my questions with a question?"

Lissa finished the sip of tea she had started. She replaced her cup with a barely discernible click. The crackers and tea were beginning to ease her stomach distress. "My family taught me to rely on God for my protection. And to stand on my own two feet."

Brent's jaw tightened almost imperceptibly. He sliced a neat cut through his steak. "Are you implying that you don't need me?"

"For protection? I'm not saying that at all. God provides protection for His own in many different ways. As a Christian you yourself should realize that. You may be one of those ways for me. It's just that I believe in being cautious." She returned to her former topic, "And in knowing a person's motives before giving my life's story to them. I may be part of a large family, but I am still a very private person when it comes to people I don't know."

Brent met her comments with silence. The slightest hint of emotion crossed his features, but Lissa couldn't decipher what those emotions were. She suspected that he was slightly irritated, and not planning to pursue the discussion any further. Along with that, however, Lissa also got the impression that Detective Brent Jamison asked a lot of questions, was probably an important man, but was...she took another sip of tea and looked up at him again...lonely?

What if God had truly sent this man into her life just now to protect her? She wondered suddenly, fleetingly, just how close Brent was to the Lord he professed to know. What if...there was a reason for her being in his life? If so....

"Do you enjoy photography?" Lissa asked.

The depth of creases around Brent's darkened eyes seemed to lessen. A moment passed while he studied her. "I do."

"Have you ever been in a photography studio...to see how the work is done, I mean."

"I've done some black and white of my own in the past."

"I see." Lissa toyed with the shreds of cellophane.

Brent held out his hand for the pieces of wrapper. She dropped the cellophane into his hand. "Eat," he said. There was a space of time while Lissa tasted a bite of her potato. A minute later, Brent admitted, "Color processing is something I've never seen. I'd enjoy a tour."

The remainder of the meal was spent in sporadic conversation of photographic interests as each of them ate.

Once she began to eat, Brent did nothing to put her on the spot. After obtaining the details of her involvement with Karl, he let the issue drop. For that, Lissa was grateful.

About the time they were done, a policeman dropped by to tell Detective Jamison—it seemed odd, somehow, to look at Brent in that capacity—the work was done at the apartment, and they would be sealing the door so no one could enter.

As the policeman turned and left, Brent returned his attention to his coffee...and to Lissa. He took a final drink, then said, "If you're ready, I'll take care of the bill."

Lissa nodded and swallowed a last bite as she rose with him.

The temperature was dropping. Lissa felt it as soon as they walked outside. She shoved her hands into the deep pockets of her coat.

The detectives were leaving the apartment by the time Brent and Lissa arrived. Several packets of articles had been confiscated, including Karl's soiled clothing and a set of small spiral notebooks Lissa recognized as Karl's daily journals. Lissa stepped aside and watched the last few adjustments to the tape barring entrance to Karl's apartment.

If there was anything for her in Karl's apartment Lissa could not hope to find it now. But, then, could there have been anything there in the first place for her to find?

Somehow, she felt certain, there was an answer here, some clue Karl had left her. But where?

"Are you ready?" Brent touched her arm and motioned for her to precede him down the hall.

Brent told her that he would follow her home, and Lissa hurried to her car, leaving Brent talking with another man who had eased his car forward as the two of them exited the apartment building. Turning on the ignition, Lissa waited, listening to the whirring of the fan as the heater began to pour out warmth.

Looking back across the parking lot, Lissa frowned. She could not see the man in the car, but she did see Brent briefly look her direction. He shook his head. His breath clouded around his face. A finger jabbed through the shadows toward the man in the car. More conversation. An additional gesture or two.

When Brent looked her way again, Lissa felt a touch of uncertain curiosity about the subject of the discussion. Her fingers crept toward the floor shift to squeeze the lock button. Lissa slid the indicator back to reverse. With a soft adjustment in motor speed, the car kicked into gear.

Brent's head bobbed up. His eyes, across the space between them, locked onto Lissa's. The palm of his hand snapped down on the roof of the car as he fired a series of comments to the man inside, then he cut around the front of the vehicle to jog toward Lissa.

Lissa rolled down her window and was about to speak when Brent said, "Head for home." She stared at his retreating figure. The man in the car drove slowly by, but it was too dark for her to see the person's features. An uneasy sensation crawled down the middle of her back, and Lissa tried unsuccessfully to shake it off.

The drive to her own apartment did not take long, but it was long enough for Lissa to begin to wonder what Brent expected of her. As she pulled into her own private garage, Lissa saw his sedan park across the street.

Lissa hurried from her garage to the foyer entrance where Brent was waiting silently. At his questioning look Lissa said, "This way." The hall was lighted, empty—and so quiet the softened whisper of their footsteps on the carpeting could be plainly heard.

"I'd like your answering machine tape," Brent said as Lissa let them into her apartment. "Karl may have left some clue you overlooked. Besides, I may need it as evidence."

"Evidence of what?" Lissa asked as she crossed the room

to her answering machine.

Brent shrugged. "Who knows what he's into?"

"Probably my answering machine." The words came out in disbelief. Lissa dropped her purse on the counter. "The tape's gone."

The machine was open, empty.

Lissa met Brent's implacable stare with one of her own.

– 11 –

"See how the color tones change?" Lissa asked as she laid a color filter over a portrait proof. "No matter how many times I do it, I'm always amazed that a blue filter takes the yellow out. See how white the gown becomes? And the flesh tones...much more natural."

"Fascinating," Brent said, then continued to experiment with different combinations of color filters. His face showed a consuming interest that Lissa knew was more than politeness. As she studied the man who sat beside her, Lissa had to wonder what it was that drove Brent Jamison to be the way he was. Although he was obviously absorbed by what he was doing, he somehow did not seem...complete. What was it that made Brent so different from any other person she knew?

Last night Brent had made certain no one was in her apartment before checking that all the doors and windows were securely closed. Earlier today, he had implied that he had stayed outside watching her apartment for the better part of the night. By all rights, Brent should be dead tired, but he remained his quiet, often blunt self all day as he watched Lissa work. Whenever she encouraged him to take part in what she was doing, he was more than willing to attempt the job...and very competently. He took well to the complexities of photography.

"'Night, Lissa," Julie said as she slipped into her coat at the end of the day. "I'll see you in the morning."

"Can you be here by 8:30 tomorrow? Cynthia will be out on a shoot and I need someone to answer the phone while I finish the black and white work."

"I'll be here," came Brent's muttered voice.

Lissa and Julie exchanged looks and Julie said, "I'll come in early," before she exited the back entrance.

Silence hung in the color lab. Lissa had not taken the time to explain to her employees why Brent spent the day with her. Not that she understood herself why he was here. She knew he was concerned for her welfare, but becoming her personal bodyguard seemed beyond what she would consider his duty. There had been no actual threat on her life, and who would know she had Karl's key?

Brent's focus went from the picture he held to Lissa's gaze. His eyes were so unusual...sometimes dark, sometimes pale. Right now they seemed to be a mix of both...and Lissa was uncertain how she felt about this man who had entered her life and suddenly decided to stay.

Lissa's chair squeaked. She placed her hands on the counter in front of her and confronted him. "You are not my nanny, you know."

"But you are my accepted responsibility."

"What do your superiors say about spending so much time with one person?"

"Nothing."

"Why should they agree to your staying with me? No

67

one's threatened me. Aren't you needed somewhere else...like out finding Karl or the person who tore his apartment apart?"

Brent's eyes darkened and the brown took over the blue. "We have people looking for Karl Karello...and the person or persons who ransacked his place." He stopped, his look intense. "Being with you is no problem. I wish all my assignments were as educational as this one. Besides, I don't mind spending time with you."

"Don't you ever smile?" The words in her mind came out before Lissa had time to consider the impact of what she had asked.

"Rarely," he said.

The one word hit Lissa with such force that she found she had no answer to his comment. Brent laid down the picture he held. His index finger touched the tip of her little finger and drew a line down the side of her hand to her wrist. It was a soft, gentle touch. "Maybe," Brent said quietly, taking his finger out of contact with her skin, "you could help me with that."

"I don't know if I can. What...are you expecting?"

There was a moment when nothing was said. Brent's lips tightened as he stood up and pushed his chair under the work counter. A hand grazed his hair. "I shouldn't have done that," he said.

"What? Touch me? Ask me to help?"

"I'm expecting absolutely nothing from you," his darkened gaze connected with hers, "except to be in your company to make certain no one harms you. As far as my superiors are concerned, you know we're in touch with one another."

"Why am I so important that you can dedicate your time exclusively to me? What are you not telling me?"

Brent's jaw tensed. "Let's go get a bite to eat. I'm hungry."

"You're avoiding my questions."

"You're right," he said, "I am." He reached for Lissa's coat hanging on a row of pegs.

Dinner was a silent affair. A relationship that had begun almost forcefully had turned into a, she supposed from Brent's final reactions, necessary alliance. The encounter had become disturbing...and Lissa struggled to know why. For some inexplicable, peculiar reason, Lissa felt drawn to Brent...to this man who shuttered his thoughts. But what was going on? With Karl...with Brent. Lissa's gaze touched Brent. What drove this man?

"Are you finished?" Brent asked. He touched the corners of his mouth and dropped the napkin on the table beside his plate.

Lissa toyed with the meal she had barely touched. "I suppose," she said.

"Not hungry?"

"I've things on my mind."

"Such as...."

Lissa's gaze moved up from her fork to study Brent's face. She had to admit this person seated across from her was handsome in a rugged, driven sort of way. His brown hair was to the dark side, full and thick. The creases alongside his mouth were deep.

When Lissa focused on his eyes she wondered how much joy Brent had known. The type of work he did must be a heavy burden...but Lissa was certain there was more to it than his work. Surely this was not the normal expression haunting detectives.

Lord, what is it about Brent? What do you want me to do? Why have you brought the two of us together?...And why am I sitting here at one of the nicest restaurants in town when I have no idea where to find Karl? Is he all right?

"Such as...?" Brent's voice demanded an answer.

69

"I'm wondering where Karl is."

Brent shrugged and gave a slight shake of his head. "Let's go," he said.

Brent had insisted on taking his car and leaving hers at the apartment. "It's easier to keep track of you this way," he had said. Now Lissa wished she had driven herself. There was nothing she wanted more than to be alone for a while...to have a chance to think clearly without Brent Jamison's presence clouding her mind.

As they drove across town, Brent remained silent, his thumb connecting rhythmically with the steering wheel. Lissa was relieved when they pulled into the lighted parking lot of her apartment complex.

When Lissa reached to unlock her apartment door, she stopped suddenly, and pushed the door with her fingertips. It moved.

"Karl!" Lissa whispered. Her look darted to Brent.

Brent's coat scraped against itself as he pulled his gun from the shoulder holster. He held the weapon upright, close to his chest.

"No!" Lissa cried, her voice restrained, horrified.

Brent snared Lissa's wrist and she nearly cried out against the pressure he was inflicting. The detective was firm, but his eyes softened. He kept his voice low, as if willing Lissa to look at him, to listen to what he had to say.

"Karl could be armed and dangerous. If he's hurting, he may not think about who else he might accidentally hurt." The pressure eased. "I'll open the door. I want you to call out, but stay behind me, away from the door."

Lissa hesitated until Brent pierced her with a stare. The look went through her, riveting her...but there was no demand. It was a request—a plea. Lissa nodded.

Brent let go. Touching the door with his elbow, he nudged it open a few inches, then looked back at Lissa.

"Karl...?" Lissa's voice was a tight sound. She tried to

see past Brent, wondering, praying that Karl would be there, that he would be safe. Brent eased the door back slowly. . .and Lissa's hands flew to stop the cry that trembled on her lips. Her apartment had been torn apart!

Furniture, books, dishes—strewn in sickening disorder—could be seen in the soft light of the lamp.

Horror overwhelmed her and Lissa started to move forward, but stopped as Brent caught her briefly with his free hand. He motioned for her to back away from the door and into the hallway.

Karl was not here. She knew that before Brent checked to make certain there was no one in the kitchen. Karl would not have destroyed her apartment like this.

But. . .who would?

Cautiously, Brent went to search Lissa's bedroom and bath. Coming back a few moments later, he moved toward the sliding glass door where cold air seeped through an inch wide crack. Easing the door back, Brent stepped through to the patio. After a minute, Lissa heard him say, "There's no one here."

Lissa hurried across the room, avoiding the items scattered about the floor, and followed the detective outside.

Cold wind whipped Lissa's hair about her face. She brushed it away and drew it back so she could see where Brent pointed at a section of broken branches on the bush below her patio.

"From the looks of it, our man went over the balcony." The detective scanned the ground below, but they could see little in the darkness. "I suspect something may have surprised him. Otherwise he would have gone out the way he came in."

"How did he know to come here?"

"Who knows?"

Lissa began to shake with cold. . .and fear. Someone knew Karl had given her the key. . . .Someone knew where she lived.

Who?

Lissa closed her eyes to the dismay that overtook her. She followed Brent's lead when he reentered her apartment, and watched as he withdrew a handkerchief and carefully closed the door behind him. The quiet emphasized the sick destruction that surrounded them.

Where are you, Karl? What are you expecting me to do? Where am I going to find him, Lord? Please don't let me be...too late. Please keep him safe...and me, too.

Brent holstered his gun and straightened his jacket. Lissa took a few steps around the room. The damage was more than she wanted to face.

"Don't touch anything," Brent said. "I want to get the lab over here as soon as possible. Whoever it was, this guy was messy. He's bound to have left something behind."

Lissa looked around her. "None of this makes sense." Then, cadence rising, "Why would anyone shoot Karl? What is going on?" Lissa's voice took on a thin edge. *"Where is Karl?"* She bit her lip and hugged her arms to herself. Lissa struggled with the sudden sensation of tears. She would not cry. Not now. Not in front of this man. She took a slow, deep breath.

Brent's voice was low. "We'll find Karl. He'll be all right."

Lissa gazed around her, taking in everything—the pillows tossed from the sofa, a broken figurine, an antique plate, miraculously still in one piece but flung onto the couch. Lissa's teeth sank into the soft flesh of her lip in an attempt to stop the tears that were beginning to form in spite of her determination.

All her belongings...someone she didn't know had gone through them, carelessly, cruelly, handling things no one else had the right to touch.

Brent came up beside her. Reaching over, he pulled her into his arms.

Lissa pressed her cheek into the scratchy wool of Brent's jacket and gave in, her tears darkening the lapel with damp, oddly shaped circles.

– 12 –

Brent's arms held her carefully. His voice was a rough rumble. "Most criminals don't care who they hurt."

"I feel so...violated...all my things...." Her head bobbed upward with surprised realization. Brent loosened his hold and looked into her eyes. "How did they know to come here?"

"My guess is whoever it was followed Karl. They probably assumed he left whatever they are looking for here, waited for a likely time to come and search, and destroyed your apartment trying to find it themselves." His expression altered slightly. "Was the key here? Did they find it?"

Lissa managed to shake her head. She swiped at the remaining tears. "I've got it."

"On you?"

She nodded and sniffed. Brent fished an unused handkerchief from his pocket and handed it to Lissa. Her mouth gave a wry twist. "Do you have an endless supply of these things?"

His raised brow was the only answer Brent gave. He shook out the handkerchief he had used earlier and walked to the telephone. When the call rang through, he requested the necessary personnel to investigate Lissa's break-in, then said to Lissa as he hung up, "After the lab people arrive, I'm taking you somewhere safe."

"Is there anyplace safe?"

Brent's darkened eyes took on a penetrating quality. "I won't let anyone hurt you."

"What about Karl?" Lissa asked.

"Until he comes forward, there isn't much we can do. The police are watching for him," he added as Lissa began to protest. "If the man wants to be found, we'll find him. If not," his tone softened, "we'll find him, anyway."

"Lissa...?"

Turning at the disbelieving quality of a feminine voice, Lissa saw her neighbor, Marlene, in the doorway, a small paper sack in her hands. She ventured a step into the apartment.

"Don't touch anything," Brent said, flashing his identification.

Marlene stopped. Her eyes were wide with unasked questions. "I heard voices," she explained, "and I knew you should be home," she lifted the bag as explanation, "so I thought you'd want your mail. I missed you the last couple days...with my schedule...and yours."

"Someone broke in," Lissa said, which hardly seemed necessary since that much was obvious. "Nothing seems to have been taken. You didn't see Karl this evening, did you?"

"Your boyfriend? No."

Brent said, "Although you may not have seen Mr. Karello this evening, can you remember any other person or anything else that may have struck you as being odd?"

"Huh-uh," Marlene started, "I—Wait a minute. Come to think of it, I may have seen something. At the time I didn't think much of it, but now I suppose it could be important. There was a guy coming in the building not long ago—when I was coming home. This man wasn't anyone I knew, and I wondered if he was the new tenant for the apartment upstairs. But I didn't watch to see where he went."

"Could you describe him to me?" Brent asked.

"I don't know," Marlene said. "He was dark—tanned, I think, with gray eyes, maybe. He didn't really look at me. But he was tall. I figure he had to be six three or four. He had brown hair—kind of curly. And he was big. I don't mean heavy, I mean big." She shifted her hands on the bag, crackling the paper as she emphasized, "Broad across the shoulders, like he was a weight lifter, or something."

"Is there anything else you can tell me?"

"I wish I had seen a car, a license plate, or something." Marlene's expression was pained. "I feel like I'm not being much help."

"You're doing fine. The man," Brent asked, "did he have any outstanding features?"

"None that I could think of. The only unusual thing about it was that I thought I'd seen this man somewhere before." Her mouth moved briefly to one side. "Probably at a grocery store. I'm certainly not into lifting weights."

While Brent questioned Marlene, trying to accumulate any other information, Lissa found herself wishing this was all a bad dream—that Karl had never been hurt, nor given her a key, nor expected protection for something she could not understand.

A number of officers arrived to take charge of the investigation and Marlene left. Lissa asked Brent, "May I get a few things before we leave?"

"As soon as the photos of your bedroom are taken you can get some clothing," Brent replied, "as long as we're careful about what you touch or pick up."

Lissa agreed, watching the efficiency with which the men

76

went to work. A police officer stood to the side of the living room, focused his camera, and snapped off a picture. He stepped to the other side of the room and repeated the process.

When the detective gave her permission to enter her bedroom, Lissa stared at her personal belongings scattered across her furniture and along the floor. Drawers had been riffled through and dumped. Her suitcases had been stripped and ripped apart, each pocket torn with a neat cut. Lissa went numb with the realization the man had used a knife.

What if she had been here?

What would have happened to her if she had been?

Brent was considerate enough to leave her alone while she picked up a few items. Not knowing how long she would have to be away from home, Lissa chose enough clothing to last several days. There was no sense in asking Brent how long it might take to find the man who did this. Or how long it would be before he considered it safe for her to come home.

"What if Karl comes back while I'm gone?" Lissa asked after dumping her clothing into a couple of shopping bags and joining Brent in the living room. She would have to see about having her cases replaced. Lissa scanned the room. How much more would she have to replace?

She still had her life.

Did Karl?

Lissa shuddered.

"Having Karl come back is a chance we'll have to take," Brent said. Sidetracked, he answered a question from one of his colleagues, then turned back to Lissa. "Let's go."

Freeway traffic rumbled by as they drove toward the heart of town. A double bottom rig, tires whining, screamed past. Lissa brushed back her hair and watched as the truck bounced over a rough piece of pavement. "Where are we going?" she asked.

"My place," came Brent's reply.

A sudden thump shook Lissa's heart. Her line of vision swung quickly to the man beside her. "What?!"

"My aunt lives on the property, so we won't be alone, if you're concerned."

"I—" Lissa's face warmed. "I didn't know—"

"I have a pretty good idea what must be going through your mind."

"Are you a mindreader, now?" That was petty. Lissa's sigh was soundless. "I'm sorry," she said.

Brent's hand tapped the turn signal up with a light click. The detective's look took her in as he glanced over his shoulder before changing lanes. "It's all right," he replied. "It's been a long day."

Lissa lapsed into silence. City lights swept by, alternately flashing light...shadow...light...shadow....

Lissa frowned, almost painfully. Her fingertips pressed to her forehead, then she let her hands drop to her lap. Her mind spun in a dozen different directions—the man beside her and his part in this confusing mess, Karl, the key, the blood, questions, questions, questions.

In the middle of all her thoughts she could not rid herself of the sight of Karl at the airport. The sight of his pale features and haunted eyes replayed itself over and over in her mind. Karl's voice echoed in her mind.

Don't trust anyone.

Karl, did that mean Brent, too? Should I not trust him, either? A frustrated grimace touched her face. *Why have you done this to me, Karl? Why didn't you go to the police? Playing Resistance was never like this.*

Lissa looked at the man beside her. Brent glanced at her, then returned his attention to his driving. His features seemed sharp and serious in the vague light from the dashboard. A hand lifted to run a finger alongside his mouth before replacing itself on the wheel.

Lissa stared out the window.

Lord, you've brought Brent Jamison—a detective—into my life. What am I supposed to do now? Is going with this man what you wanted me to do? I could just as easily have stayed at Marlene's or Cynthia's...but I didn't think about it then. Is this what you want? Can I trust Brent?

Brent signaled again and exited off the freeway. He negotiated several turns to weave through an older section of town. A bit of surprise sifted through Lissa as she watched stately brick homes slip by.

Once, out of curiosity, she had driven through these winding, hilly streets and was awed by the impression the older, picturesque homes evoked...as if they were suspended in a period of quieter, more tranquil times.

Brent actually lived here?

Brent turned up a paved driveway past brick columns and low walls. Ancient oak trees strained their gnarled arms out to dapple the expanse of lawn with darker, shadowed recesses. Just before the driveway swung toward the back of the house, Lissa noticed a light glowing from a window on the far side of the lower level of the two-story Tudor home.

Tall hedges, gloomy in the night, sheltered the back yard from view. Lissa watched, twitters fluttering in her midsection, as the garage door hummed its way upward, then down. She and Brent made their way to the back door of the house.

Fine gravel on the concrete drive crunched under the soles of Lissa's shoes. She attempted to ignore the eerie, gritty, echoing sound from Brent's feet. A breeze swirled around the corner of the house, teasing the ends of her hair and creeping down the back of her neck.

Lissa shifted the small sack of mail she carried. The crackling noise was loud in the whispering silence around them. With her free hand she drew her collar closer to her

79

cheeks. Brent carried the larger sack.

Subdued and dark, the house provoked an uneasy nervousness in Lissa. An overhead light flooded the room they entered to expose a large kitchen. Brent urged Lissa forward. They went through a formal dining room, past a sitting room and modest library, to a smaller room off to one side.

Quiet classical music could be heard through the open doorway. An older woman, her hair brown, but streaked with light strands of gray, sat in a corner chair. A lamp shone on her handwork. The woman smiled and rose, placing her handiwork on her seat as Lissa and Brent entered the room. "Brent...I didn't expect you to drop by this evening." Her glance, thorough, but not unkind, trailed over Lissa. "Do come in. Sit down."

"I've things to do, Aunt Enid. This is Lissa McIntyre. Would you mind seeing she has the spare bedroom? I'll be at the guest house if you need me."

Lissa's mouth dropped. "But I thought," she started and stopped, then added, "this was your house."

"It is." His look was unreadable. "Since my hours are never regular, I prefer to use the guest house. That keeps me from disturbing Aunt Enid with my coming and going." He relinquished the sack he carried, excused himself, and left the way he had come.

The room was quiet...except for the muted strains of a single violin, its poignant sounds hovering in the air. There was a space of time as the women studied one another—the older woman composed, Lissa clutching her sacks of mail and clothing.

"I must apologize for Brent." Aunt Enid's voice was soft. A forgiving smile came to her face. "He has a heart of gold, but he can be abrupt at times. Come," she said, indicating the direction Lissa should follow. "I'll take you to the guest room so you can put your things away."

The room was up a flight of stairs and to the back of the house. They traveled a long hallway lit by the glow of a single covered ceiling light.

"I hope this will be all right for you," Aunt Enid said as she stood back so Lissa could enter ahead of her. The room was pleasant, done in rose to accent the dark mahogany.

"It's fine, thank you," Lissa assured the older woman. "I'm sorry about coming unannounced. You see," her mind raced over the reasons for her being where she was, and she knew she couldn't explain everything, "Brent felt I would be...safer here."

"You don't have to explain. This isn't the first time I've had an unexpected guest in Brent's home. Would you like to join me for something to eat? I usually have a small snack before retiring for the evening."

"I think I'd rather try to get some sleep. It's been a long day."

"If you decide you need anything, please make yourself at home. Brent always comes in through the back door, so I'm certain you know where the kitchen is. The bathroom is back down the hall."

Lissa nodded. She had seen the room.

"You are welcome to use the alarm clock in the top bureau drawer, if you need to," Aunt Enid smiled. "And don't hesitate to ask if you have any questions."

"I won't," Lissa replied. She watched as the older woman left. Her retreating steps were silent until she began to descend the stairway. One creak sounded as the woman's weight touched a step somewhere midway down.

Lissa stayed still several seconds longer, until she knew Aunt Enid would have gone about her business. Lips tightening, they drew to a straight line before relaxing with an expression of resigned submission.

Placing her sacks on the bed, Lissa walked over to the room's only window. The view overlooked a small sloping portion of the roof and into the dully lit backyard where she spied a glow in a small house...the guest house.

Lissa had not noticed the building when they pulled in, due to the height of the bushes separating it from direct exposure to the main house. Brent's silhouette flashed across a large window. She watched as he removed his jacket and hung it over the back of a chair. He ran his hands through his hair. Lissa experienced a vague, uneasy feeling about watching him. Even in silhouette, she could see the shoulder holster and gun and was not certain whether seeing that made her feel safe or not. Coming from a family of five brothers, three of whom were hunters, she had a healthy respect for firearms. But hunting pheasant or deer was not the same as hunting a...a man.

Karl.

Detective Brent Jamison was hunting her childhood friend *Karl*. He was using her to lure Karl to him.

Then what?

Lissa reached up and tugged the shade down. Delicate curtains fluffed, then hung motionless. With shaky fingers, Lissa removed the long coat she wore and draped it over the end of the bed.

What had she done in allowing this man to bring her to this house?

– 13 –

Two days passed; Lissa was still at Aunt Enid's. Even though Lissa had obtained permission to return to her apartment, Brent felt it best for the time being for her to stay where she was. She had agreed. Why, however, she was not certain.

She knew she had come to accept Brent's presence. She could not fault him on his manners or his way of treating her or his willingness to be of help at the studio or on location. Yet, it was obvious he was not a contented man and for that reason alone, Lissa prayed. At times she was not certain what she prayed for, but she continued to commit all the circumstances she had gone through and those she would come up against to her Lord, trusting His sovereignty in the end to make everything come out right.

Aunt Enid was a quiet and efficient hostess, and Lissa began to feel comfortable around her. Whenever Lissa was there, they talked about a variety of topics. But Brent seemed to be one they never ventured toward in any great detail.

Dinner earlier tonight had been a modest affair with Aunt Enid in the kitchen. Lissa appreciated the simple food after the restaurants of the previous days. Not that Brent had not chosen well. He had. But Lissa enjoyed the simpleness of creating a sandwich in the quiet of a comfortable kitchen.

Although Brent had been gone earlier, Lissa knew he was home now. She had heard the sound of his car pulling into the drive. Rather than come into the main house, though, Brent went directly to the guest house. Since that was not his normal habit, it disturbed her, but Lissa realized why when, a little later, another car pulled up. She glanced out one of the bay windows and saw a man disappear around the end of the hedge.

Lissa shrugged and spread out on the table the mail Marlene had saved while Lissa was in Colorado. Lissa should have gotten to it before now, but sorting through bills and junk mail was not an undertaking she looked forward to doing.

Aunt Enid retired to the sitting room for the evening and when the telephone rang Lissa ignored it, knowing Brent's aunt would answer on the extension.

Lissa dropped a letter in a small pile and laid another advertisement on the throwaway items. Lifting a crumpled, empty envelope she glanced at the figures penned across the front...her mailbox combination. Now that Lissa was home Marlene had had no need to keep it. Lissa placed the envelope on top of the advertisement.

"There's a phone call for you," Aunt Enid said from the doorway. "The woman said her name was Julie."

Lissa hesitated. It was strange that Julie would call...particularly this late at night. She voiced her thanks to Aunt Enid and reached for the kitchen telephone.

"Lissa...Julie. I'm at the office."

"Is anything wrong?"

"I'm not sure. Something might be right. I stopped by to

84

pick up some things I'd forgotten earlier and was here when the telephone rang. The answering machine picked up the message, but I stayed long enough to listen. A man wants you to call. He sounded...well, the only way I can put it is...really strange. In view of what's happened lately I thought you'd want to know. Have you got a piece of paper?"

"Just a minute." Lissa scanned the piles on the table and grabbed the envelope she'd laid aside. Propping the phone under her chin, she smoothed the envelope with the heel of her hand, then picked up a pen. "Okay," she said. "What's the number?"

"555-8734. Do you recognize it?"

"I don't, but it might just be what we've been waiting for," Lissa responded, scribbling the numbers below the mailbox combination. "Thanks, Julie," she said and hung up before the receptionist could reply.

Her nervous fingers managed to punch out the numbers. Lissa listened impatiently. She glanced at the envelope in her hand and prayed. This had to be Karl. It just *had* to be.

"Knight's Inn," a coarse male voice spoke.

"Mr. Karello's room, please."

"Ain't nobody here by that name."

Disappointment shook Lissa. "Are you sure?" she asked.

"'Course I'm sure." The voice sounded annoyed.

Now what?

Resistance.

What was she thinking? Of course Karl wouldn't be using his own name. "What about..." Her mind spun. What had Karl used? "...Holmes—Richard Holmes?"

A pause, then, "Sure," the voice said.

Lissa drew in a sharp breath of mingled disbelief and thankfulness. Dead silence filled the line, then a click, then ringing.

Finally.

85

Her hands shook. Lissa half-laughed at herself for her reaction. Now, maybe, her questions would be answered.

The phone continued to ring. Lissa shifted her position. *Not now. Please, Karl, be there.*

Karl has to be okay. Dear God, make him answer the phone.

Two more rings.

Why doesn't he answer the phone?

A voice cut in, not Karl's—the office manager, his throaty sounds grating on her ear. "He don't seem to be in. Do you wanta leave a message?"

A half-formed plan began to take shape in Lissa's mind. "Where are you located?"

The man gave an address, one that under ordinary circumstances Lissa would never frequent at night. She jotted it down.

Lissa hung up the phone...and stopped. She had no car. Brent did.

Aunt Enid reentered the kitchen, and Lissa said, "I've got to talk with Brent. It's very important," and left by the back door. The outer storm door snapped back with a bang as she turned to close it.

Cold wind whipped into the yard, swirling icy fingers through her clothing. Shriveled leaves spun about in a dry, rustling rain. Lissa was grateful for the bulky sweater she wore...and realized she should have taken the time to grab a coat. Hugging her arms to herself, Lissa tucked the envelope close to her body.

The path to the guest house was a circular design of brick that ran around the far end of the hedges. Hunching her shoulders, Lissa hurried past a series of short, decorative landings and up two stairs to the front patio. Pausing to catch her breath, she started to rap on the glassed portion of the door...and stopped.

Voices could be heard through the door—loud voices, both

male. Lissa wavered, wondering whether she should knock anyway. Karl was too important to wait.

Shadows crossed the portion of the entry area she could see through the sheer curtains, and, inexplicably, Lissa shied away.

"Miss McIntyre is in my..." she heard.

McIntyre...? Her?

"...won't appreciate you making his decisions for him."

"I didn't ask whether he would or not."

Lissa's heart began a deep, steady rhythm. She leaned as close to the door as she dared.

"He'll have to be patient and wait this thing out. There's nothing more we can do at this point."

The shadows moved again, flickering an indistinct dance on the floor. She strained to hear more. There were more indistinct words, then, "It's going to be done my way," one voice stated flatly. "You're not going to...." Lissa lost the words as they trailed off.

Lissa's heart accelerated. What was going on?

"We are in this together."

That was Brent. He continued to talk. "Don't be stupid. You hurry this and play it wrong and you..." the words muffled. Lissa pursed her lips with frustration, then heard very distinctly, "...get us all killed!"

Lissa's heart made an intensified jump. What were these two men talking about?

Lissa crept to the front window. Her hands steadied themselves against the cold, rough brick facing. Her mouth was dry.

"Stay out of it, Hanson." Lissa heard. "I have the girl and she has what we need. I need time. She doesn't understand what she's into, and if I can get the information without her knowing, there's no reason for her to be hurt. She doesn't realize who's involved—"

"She doesn't suspect?"

"My position, his position...both are secure."

Lissa could make out the back of Brent's head. He moved out of sight. She inched closer.

More conversation, then, distinctly, "Is that a threat?" Brent had turned back. His face was twisted with intense emotion. His eyes became points of gray and blue glittering in their background of brown.

"You do what I said or I come get the girl."

Lissa swallowed a sound of dismay. The man who spoke was tall—over six foot, curly dark hair, broad shoulders. Her breath came in tiny, silent gasps. The man matched Marlene's description!

"You can't kill her!" Brent's hand sliced the air.

The other man's lip curled in contempt. "Better her than me. I'm not taking the rap for your stupidity!"

"We'll all be prosecuted."

"Not me! They may get *you*," Hanson's heavy finger jabbed at Brent, then swung wide and snapped toward himself, "but *I'm* not getting burned! I'll get that information with or without your help, and without pussyfooting around waiting for you to play Mr. Good Cop!"

Lissa recoiled and flattened against the house. Her breath came in quick snaps. Dizzy streaks swirled through her head. She struggled, attempted to clear her mind.

...waiting for you to play Mr. Good Cop!

Lissa was moving, hurrying down the steps, across the yard. She veered away from the house, around it, through the yard.

Crooks...this man, Hanson...Brent?...Aunt Enid? Was she one of them? That innocent woman? No!

I'm a Christian, too...

I'll protect you.

Lies.

Was everything Brent had told her...all lies? She wanted to cry. Brent was a...a *liar*. He had deceived her, strung her along for...for *what*?

Lissa raced under the spreading arms of the oak trees. The sound of a car motor stopped her short. She flung herself behind the trunk of a large tree and cowered there, hardly daring to look as the headlights' twin beams pierced the length of the drive.

It was the car—the gray car—she had seen in the parking lot at Karl's apartment...the man in the shadows talking with Brent. Why hadn't she noticed the car before? Had this man followed Karl to her apartment? Was he the same person who tore Karl's apartment apart? Had he been the one to...to shoot Karl?

Turning onto the street, the car gunned its engine and raced down the block.

Lissa half walked, half ran. She had to get away. Somewhere else, anywhere, so she could get her thoughts together. She clambered over the low wall, scraping her hands and nearly losing her balance. Scrambling upright, Lissa hurried on, her breath coming in short sobs.

Brent...was part of this...horror.

Lissa endured the wave of betrayal that surged over her.

Oh, God! What am I doing? How could you allow me to begin to trust that man? Where should I go? What should I do?

Resistance! I've failed Karl. What if I get him killed?

She had to find Karl. She had the address. Her fingers tightened on the crushed envelope in their grip.

Chill wind bit her face, cut through her sweater. She shook with cold. A car came toward her. Lissa sidestepped into a driveway, behind a bush. The headlights swept past as the vehicle turned down a side street.

Her hair blew around her face. She should have taken a coat. Lissa tugged her sweater around her throat. The envelope crackled in her hand. She started down a short hill.

Once out of the housing area she could locate a quick-stop shop and telephone...who? Calling the police was out of the question. They'd never believe her wild accusations about Brent. What proof did she have that he was crooked? An overheard conversation? It was her word against his.

Could she get in trouble for eavesdropping through a window?

Lissa prayed Cynthia would be home.

She heard the sound of a car before the headlights broke the crest of the hill behind her. Dashing in among a grouping of trees, Lissa held her breath and waited. With a quick glance around she saw she was close to another driveway, a long one. A house back in the trees had lights glowing, warm, shining from almost every window.

The car moved slowly...and she recognized it.

– 14 –

Light and shadow played odd colors down the car's sleek body as it slowly moved in and out of the street lights.

Lissa nearly wept. She waited, hardly daring to breathe. The car came to a stop. Lissa sought the house behind her. If she could run fast enough...stay behind enough trees....Could they hear her if she screamed?

"Lissa..." Brent's low voice carried through the soughing wind. The car was still running. He stood alongside it. What was he doing?

Suddenly a light began to flash—a portable beacon revolving round and round, flashing spears of light into the street, across the bushes, into the trees. Brent was moving around the car. "I know you're there. Please don't run."

How did he know where she was? Lissa looked down and gave a sharp gasp. The sleeve of her sweater trailed to the side of the tree, the teal glowing with a peculiar color every time the light circled. She snapped her elbow to herself, jerking the betraying fabric from the light.

"Come on out," he said. "I won't hurt you."

Won't hurt me? What killer would tell her otherwise?

She heard again in her mind that man—Hanson—asking, *She doesn't suspect?*

My position is secure.

Was it possible?...Could it be...that *Brent* had been... the one to shoot Karl? Lissa's mind spun with the memory of Karl's face, the sound of his pained voice, Brent's voice saying, ...*not what we would consider a flesh wound.*

With a desperate lunge Lissa sprinted into a run. She heard Brent's low shout. The house lay straight ahead.

Lissa's feet pounded on the leaf-covered grass. She ducked under a branch, skirted a tree. Limbs snatched at her hair, tore at her sweater.

Brent would show his identification, she realized, and say he was the police. She had to plead with them to call someone else...anyone other than—

A fierce blow to the back of her knees brought her down, and she went rolling, leaves crackling and bodies heaving tortured gasps.

Lissa came alive, swinging and kicking. She had not been raised with five brothers without learning some form of self defense. She would not be taken without a fight.

Brent gave an exclamation of pained surprise when her fist connected with his chin. Lissa slipped free, crawling hastily, trying to stand. He snared her foot, tripped her, and she rolled, giving a kick to free his grip. But he was after her, moving quicker than she could stand, his hand encircling her ankle, snatching at her waist.

Lissa's scream was cut to a violent expulsion of air as Brent's arm jerked her around by her midsection. "Lissa!" he demanded. "Stop it! I'm not going to hurt you!"

"Like you didn't hurt Karl?" She swung with her shoulders, attempting to disconnect the man who was pinning her arms behind her as he hauled her upright. "I don't want to hear your lies!" She kicked, but her heels struck only air.

"It's not like you think. I didn't shoot Karl. I tried to help him. I'm only trying to help you. Ouch! Stop it!"

Lissa sucked in a deep breath. The earsplitting sound was smothered by the width of Brent's hand before it began. His other arm snapped around her middle, pulling her hard against himself. "Stop it, Lissa," Brent's voice grated at her ear. "I'm an undercover agent working on a sting operation. I didn't shoot Karl, but I know who did."

Undercover cop? This was crazy! He was pretending to be a cop gone bad?

"Please believe me," Brent said. "I'm telling the truth."

Lissa hesitated, trying to decide whether to trust him.

Brent's grip eased fractionally. "I'm going to take my hand away. Let's go back to the car and we'll talk." His hand removed itself slowly, cautiously, from her mouth.

Lissa stared at the house, willing someone to come out. No one seemed to have taken note of the flashing light. The wind lifted and tossed the leaves at their feet. Somewhere a dog had started to bark, a wailing type of howl, but it was some distance away.

"We'll talk here," Lissa said, her voice rough.

"Fair enough." Brent's grip loosened.

Lissa hissed a breath into her lungs. "Who shot Karl?"

"I can't tell you that. The less you know the better—for your own sake."

"That's absurd! Don't you think I'm in enough danger now as it is?" Long strands of hair blew across her face and she brushed them away in exasperation. "Shouldn't I at least know what's going on?"

"I'm not at liberty to tell you." He gripped her arm. "Let's get out of here."

"No!" Lissa jerked away.

Brent stopped still, hands snapped back, away from his body. His eyes glittered in the weird flashing scene. "I don't

93

blame you for not trusting me, Lissa. I'm certain what you heard was very condemning, so I want to make it clear that I'm not going to force you to go anywhere with me. I won't even ask for the key Karl gave you. You can go."

"Just like that?" Lissa could not stop the small amount of bitterness that came out with her words. Prickles of pain ran the length of her body, protesting his mistreatment.

Hands slowly dropping, Brent watched her. He had added an overcoat to his clothing. The collar lifted in the wind and touched the side of his face, once, twice.

"Just like that," he repeated slowly. His jaw was tight, his mouth a grim line, but his eyes....

Lissa stared at this man who was silently pleading with her to accept what he said, to have faith in him, to willingly —blindly—entrust her safety into his care.

Lord...I have a choice to make—and I don't know what to do. You heard the argument back at the house. You know this man in front of me. You know if he belongs to you or whether that's a lie too. You've searched his heart, but all I have is his word. I need to know what to do. He's giving me the chance to walk away. Do I leave or go with him? I need some direction. Father, help me! I'm your child and I know you won't let anything happen to me that's not in your plan, but you've got to help me know. I don't know what to do.

Brent's hand slowly turned over and lifted toward her. His eyes begged her to take it.

Lissa waited until...a small peace of acceptance settled through her. Was this what she was looking for?

Lissa lifted her chin. Brent's hand remained steady, waiting, his eyes...watching.

Is this it, Father? Am I to trust this man in spite of everything I've seen and heard?

Her fingers stretched out and touched his. The grip that tightened drew her close.

A sigh of relief came from Brent. "You don't know how I prayed you'd believe me," he said.

"You don't know how I prayed to know whether or not I should."

"No matter what happens from here on out, I need you to do exactly as I say. Your life could depend on it. And if anything happens to me, go directly to Detective Sidney Bendar at police headquarters. Got that?"

"Detective Bendar, police headquarters."

"You must trust me—explicitly, without question."

Locked by his gaze, Lissa nodded. "I'll...try."

Brent accepted Lissa's words. He turned, leading her back to the car. "Let's go to the house. You're freezing."

Lissa pulled back. "We can't. Karl's at Knight's Inn, d-downtown."

Brent stopped and flashed his probing glance across Lissa's features.

"Julie called. There was a m-message for me. That's why I was at the guest house—to tell you." Then, "I've lost the envelope," she realized suddenly. "The one with the address...when we f-fought."

"I know where Knight's Inn is located."

But Lissa spied a bit of paper almost buried in the leaves. She snatched at it. It was the envelope.

"Come on," Brent retook her arm and hustled toward the car. He gestured, indicating that she should get in as he took the light from the roof of the car.

"What's this all about?" Lissa asked. "I have the right to know," she emphasized over the slamming of doors. "And d-don't tell me the less I know the better, because it isn't true. Ignorance could get me into a lot more trouble. Not knowing just how you fit into the scheme of things d-didn't help much this evening, now did it?"

But Brent ignored Lissa's comments and questions, except to say, "I can't tell you anything. Believe me," he clicked on the heater, "if I could tell you, I would. But if you knew," his voice became grim, "it wouldn't set your mind at ease."

"You make it s-sound...so horrible."

She could see Brent's jaw tighten. A frown drew his brows together. "I've seen the results of ruthlessness. It's not pretty."

Lissa hesitated, watching this man beside her. She reached out to touch Brent's sleeve. "I'm sorry."

His look took in first her hand, then her face. Lissa bore his scrutiny.

"For what?" he asked. "Because I chose to become a police detective?"

"For disbelieving you...and for whatever it is...that...seems to have hurt you so much."

Brent made a small noise. He pulled away from the curb.

"You say you're a Christian, Brent. Have you forgotten what that means? Or did you ever really know?"

"What's that supposed to mean?"

"Have you really trusted Jesus Christ as your Lord and Savior?"

Brent gave a sigh and there was silence. The heater poured out warmth and the tires hummed along the streets. Brent stared at the road ahead. They passed through a series of intersections. The residential area was left behind.

"Years ago," Brent said finally. "Years ago when I was young and naive. A fifteen-year-old boy not disillusioned by power and greed and the evil in the world—yes. I trusted in Jesus Christ to save me from my sins and make everything right."

"Don't you believe Him anymore?"

"Sometimes it's hard. Oh, I know He's saved me," Brent's hand lifted with a gesture, "but there are times I see things happen and I have to question, 'Why'?"

"We all have those times," Lissa said. "Although *you* may know, I can't understand why someone is after me or why

96

I'm going through this with Karl."

"What *is* your relationship to Karl? What does he mean to you?"

Lissa blinked at the suddenness of the question. "Are you jealous?"

"There you go again."

"What are you talking about?"

"Answering my question—"

"—with a question. Well, are you?"

"You aim for the jugular, don't you?"

"Karl Karello is a dear friend I grew up with. We've had special times together, but neither of us are interested in the other as anything but close friends. He asked me to play a game of Resistance with him. It's a game we played as children," she explained at his look. "I'm afraid the result of this 'game' may have deadly consequences. Now I'm trying to find him. Does that answer your question?"

"We're here," Brent said. He pointed. Just ahead "Knight's Inn" glowed vertically in orange neon light. He slipped into a parallel parking spot a half block away from the motel.

Brent said, "Stay here."

"I'm coming with you." Lissa replied, her car door already open.

"I don't want to argue with you—"

"Then don't. I'm going to Karl."

Lissa was already half out of her seat when Brent snared her arm. "You'll be safer in the car." Brent's look pierced her own.

"While we sit here disagreeing," Lissa said, tugging against his grip, "Karl could be dying. Let *go*," she uttered with one last unsuccessful attempt to pull her arm free.

Glints of blue from Brent's eyes sparked in the street light. "You are the most determined, obstinate—"

"Yes," she agreed. "I'm constantly battling those traits. I confess them to God more often than I care to admit." Her tone dropped dramatically. "Now...can we please go?"

Brent let loose a slow heave of resignation. "Stay close to me, do exactly as you are told, and don't do anything foolish." He released his hold with one final look. Lissa, not giving him time to reconsider, hurriedly exited, and quietly closed the door.

The overweight man behind the counter at Knight's Inn gave a cursory glance over his grimy reading glasses when Brent and Lissa walked through the front door. The bell above the door tinged again as the door swung back shut.

A fissured black leather sofa in the tiny lobby was splattered with newspapers. An unshaven, sour-faced old man perched his bony body in a chair near the reception counter. Diverting his attention from a piece of ragged newsprint, he speared Lissa and the detective in his unwavering scrutiny. Lissa edged closer to Brent.

The smells that assaulted her were nauseating—the dirt and stench of unwashed bodies, the smoke, aerosols, and other odors she could not, nor wanted to name. From somewhere the sounds of a television drifted into the room...and argumentative voices—a man and a woman, the woman's voice taking on a shrill escalating pitch.

Brent asked, "Which room is Karl Karello occupying?"

"Not Karello," Lissa inserted, "Richard Holmes."

"Well, now," the fat man behind the counter straightened and ran his dirty nails under his suspenders to idly scratch his belly. "Who would you be that you'd be wantin' ta know?"

Other than to stay as close as possible, Lissa paid little attention to Brent showing his identification and requesting information. The steady scrutiny of the old man sitting in the lobby had her skin crawling. She stared back as long as she dared, hoping to show a brave front that was in no way a reality. But the inscrutable dark eyes remained unblinkingly focused on her.

"Hey," the man behind the counter said abruptly, bringing Lissa's attention back to him. "We run a clean place here. Don't give me no threats."

"Then show us the room." Brent's gaze was direct, his voice inflexible, mouth tight, expressionless. "And bring the master key in case he doesn't come to the door."

The heavy man grumbled and reached to a slot behind him, withdrawing a yellow piece of cardboard which was attached to a key.

"No matter if'n this guy done somethin' wrong, we still got us a clean place here. You got no cause ta look no place else but this here Mr. Holmes's room."

"Of course," Brent murmured. He took Lissa's arm and followed the man down a hallway and up a narrow flight of sagging stairs.

The arguing voices had heightened to a constant barrage, and the clerk slammed a fist on a door as he passed, saying, "Pipe down, or I'm sendin' in the cops!" There was a brief moment of silence, then the noise continued at a lower level. "This is the one," he said, coming to another door.

Rusting numbers on a yellowed and paint-chipped door spelled out 12.

– 15 –

Unable to restrain herself, Lissa pounded her fist against the door. It shook under her efforts.

"Karl! It's Lissa. Open the door!"

Nothing. Absolutely nothing.

Brent rattled the doorknob, then gestured. "Open it," he ordered. The clerk did...and the door swung back three inches to be stopped by a chain.

Lissa could see light, a part of a wall. "*Please*," she said, grappling at Brent's sleeve.

Brent gave the order to, "Stand back," propelling Lissa away from the doorway with a directing hand. As a precautionary measure, he drew his pistol. Intent darkened Brent's eyes with determination, and his mouth slimmed to a fine line. Brent took a step, then kicked his foot out with a solid blow...and the door slammed open, the safety chain yanking plaster from the wall as it snapped back.

"Karl!" A sobbing cry tore from Lissa's throat as she lunged toward the sagging double bed and the crumpled figure of a man. Lissa was stopped by Brent's restraining hand. He gave a careful, measuring glance around the sorry room, then hurried ahead.

Lissa slid to her knees beside the bed, her hands out, but fearing to touch this man. His gray features almost bore no resemblance to the Karl she knew. His eyes were closed, sunken, his breathing very shallow. Brent took one look and ordered the clerk to, "Call an ambulance."

"That didn't happen here," the man said, indicating Karl's condition.

"We know," Brent replied.

"You'll pay for the door," the man added.

"Fine." There was a commanding crispness to Brent's voice. "It's covered. Now call the ambulance."

"We run a clean place here," the fading voice insisted as the man went back down the hall.

"Karl," Lissa whispered, "I got your message. I'm here. Oh, *Karl*...." She took in the details of his stained clothing and haggard face. A makeshift bandage could be seen through the opening of his shirt. His hand was clammy. "How did this happen? How could something like this possibly happen?"

Brent put away his gun. "The ambulance will be here soon. He'll have a chance if he can hold on." Lissa looked up when a hand rested itself on her shoulder. "I've seen worse," he said.

Lissa's head shook in disbelief. Her glance flicked from Brent to Karl's pinched features. In her heart she wondered if Karl could survive, and the thought tore at her soul...but she did not voice her treacherous thoughts. Instead she waited.

And Brent waited, silently, placing himself as a guard at the door.

Eventually the ambulance arrived. Paramedics fussed over Karl, checking vitals, attaching tubes, working with haste to lift him to the stretcher. Lissa watched the illusion being acted out in front of her. It had to be a horrible nightmare. How could it be reality?

People peered from doorways as Lissa numbly followed the paramedics down the hallway and onto the street. Brent was beside her—a solid form that answered questions and gave directions and said, "I'll take her," when the driver asked if Lissa needed transportation to the hospital.

The drive to the hospital was accomplished in silence. Once there, Lissa permitted Brent to lead her to Emergency where she answered questions about Karl.

By the time she was done, she was ready to sit in the quiet of the waiting room. Her numbed senses refused to allow the truth of Karl's situation to penetrate her mind. She had known Karl was hurt. Brent had warned her the wound was serious. She had seen the blood on her carpet. But hearing the words...and seeing the reality....

Brent brought coffee and placed it in Lissa's hands, then he disappeared, saying something about calls he needed to make. Lissa paid little attention to what Brent said, but sat, staring at nothing in particular, praying desperately that Karl would live.

By the time Brent returned, Lissa's untouched coffee had grown cold. He replaced it with another. His own he set on the low table in front of them so he could draw out two wrapped sandwiches he had tucked under his arm.

Lissa saw Brent peel back the cellophane. He handed one of the sandwiches to her.

"I'm not hungry."

"You need to eat. Try it. I've had them before. For hospital food, they're not bad."

"How much longer will the doctors be?"

Brent could only shrug. "They're doing everything possible to save him." He sank his teeth into his sandwich.

"I keep wondering if God will heal him. What possible

102

good can come of Karl's death?"

The look Brent gave her was solemn. "He's not dead yet."

Lissa allowed the words to flow over her, through her. Minutes passed. Lissa asked, "How much time do I have left?"

"Until what?"

"Until your man Hanson comes looking for me."

Brent swallowed the bite he had taken. He watched Lissa. "I'll hold him off."

"What happens when he won't wait any longer?"

Brent's face was dour. "You become hunted game for any of a small number of men in this part of the country."

"I'll be on a hit list," Lissa said.

"That's right."

"You don't pull any punches, do you?"

"You wouldn't have wanted me to lie."

Lissa studied his direct look. He was right. "Do you think Karl will survive?"

Brent opened his mouth to speak and hesitated. Conflict trailed across his face. "I'm not an expert," he said finally. "He's strong, though. He wouldn't have made it this long if he wasn't."

"Yes," she agreed slowly, "Karl's always been strong."

"You, too. Most women would be in hysterics by now."

Lissa made a sober sound. Her head shook slowly. "You have no idea how weak I am. I am an argumentative, headstrong woman who cries at the drop of a hat. Without Jesus Christ I have no strength."

"It's been a long time," Brent began, his voice low, "since I've remembered that Jesus Christ is my strength."

"Miss McIntyre..."

Lissa looked up to see a doctor. She was on her feet in an instant, the sandwich and coffee hastily deposited on the table in front of her. "I'm Lissa McIntyre."

"Karl is being transferred to ICU," the doctor said. "He

103

survived the surgery, but he's not out of danger yet." The doctor's brows lifted. "He's a fighter, which is good, but he's lost a lot of blood and there's a serious infection."

"He'll make it," Lissa said. "He's got to."

The doctor's gaze locked with her own. "The next twenty-four hours will tell us a lot," he answered, adding, "Would you like to see him?"

Lissa's heart jumped. "May I?"

"Five minutes is all I can offer."

"I'll take it."

Lissa looked at Brent...and was shocked to see...he was...*smiling*? It was small, barely existent, but...*true*. The lines around his mouth eased back and softened. The wonder of it stopped Lissa for a brief moment. She reached out...and his hand met hers halfway.

The doctor led the two of them through a set of double doors, down a short hall, and around a corner. Surprise struck Lissa when she saw a man—obviously not a doctor—standing outside Karl's room. He was a big man, tall and formidable. At directives from Brent the man stood aside and permitted Lissa's entrance. Brent stayed behind.

Karl was pale. A cold mosaic of tubes strung their way from his body to an assortment of steadily beeping machines.

The man on the bed still showed little likeness to the Karl Lissa knew...but it was him. His eyes were closed. She had not expected otherwise. His face under his beard was drawn, but not nearly so pinched as earlier. There was even a vague spot of color toward the outside edges of his cheekbones. She took Karl's hand in her own. It was warm, almost to the point of fevered, but, thank goodness, not cold like at the motel.

Karl had survived. Lissa breathed a fervent prayer of thanksgiving for God's mercy. Karl had walked close in the shadow of the valley, but now, she knew, he was heading for the mountaintop.

– 16 –

As the days passed, Karl showed little change. At first his condition weakened, but then he improved, if only slightly. Although he had regained a semblance of consciousness, Karl had not yet had any noticeable lucid moments. His mutterings were incoherent comments that defied understanding. The doctors reminded Lissa it would take time for Karl's body and mind to recover from the loss of blood and shock, and the infection defied any medication they administered. Yet, from all indications, Karl was holding his own, and the doctors assured Lissa the day would come that Karl would realize who she was.

After the first few days, Karl was moved from ICU to a private room. His guard went with him, which did not surprise Lissa. Whatever secret Karl knew was important enough to continue insuring his protection.

Because Lissa knew the threat to her own life was real as well, she made no suggestion about returning to her own apartment. And she did not question the fact that Brent never brought the subject up.

Although not an overly demonstrative man, Lissa realized Brent had begun to show his attention toward her in subtly noticeable ways. Since the night they found Karl, he had been less abrasive. Still blunt, she supposed he would remain that way. But he was improving.

Lissa also saw the beginnings of spiritual change in Brent that led her to believe he wanted to be close to the Lord he had accepted so many years ago. He never told her his reasons for turning cold toward God, but from their discussions Lissa received the impression the reasons centered around his father's health and something to do with past family business practices.

Aunt Enid often found time to visit with her in the evenings after Brent left for the guest house. These times were special to Lissa. She had quickly learned that Aunt Enid also knew Jesus Christ as her Savior. In fact, Aunt Enid was the person who had led Brent to a knowledge of who Jesus Christ was and the sacrifice He willingly gave for Brent's sake.

"Brent was nearly sixteen when he was saved." Aunt Enid placed her teacup into its saucer with a careful click. Her fingers picked at the corner of a linen napkin laying beside her cup and saucer. "For a year or so he was enthusiastic about church and the things of God. Then there was trouble." Aunt Enid paused. "Has Brent told you about when he left home?"

"No." Lissa laced her fingers and leaned her chin into her knuckles as her elbows connected with the table top.

"It was a troublesome time. He was barely seventeen. He and his father disagreed about something. Brent went out on his own."

Lissa's hands lowered away from her chin. "He *quit school?*"

"Even at seventeen, Brent had enough good sense not to

quit school. I don't know how he did it, but he found an apartment, studied days, worked nights. His father never notified the school about the situation. The authorities didn't find out for months. About the time they did, I discovered what Brent had done and kept him from going to a foster home." Her brows lifted briefly. "He had guts, that kid did."

Lissa smiled at the terms Aunt Enid used. "What happened then?" she asked.

"Eventually Brent and his father started speaking again. They grew quite close, in fact. Except for the decision Brent made to go into law enforcement rather than the family business, Roland had little bad to say about his son. I think there was even a bit of pride over Brent's determined will to survive on his own."

The grandfather clock in the living room struck ten, each strike a resonate, mellow sound.

"Time for me to go to bed," Aunt Enid said as she laid her hands flat on the table and shoved her chair back.

"Me, too," Lissa agreed reluctantly. "I have a busy day ahead of me tomorrow."

Aunt Enid raised her voice slightly to be heard above the sound of running water as she rinsed her cup. "Don't you go back to Walter and Olivia's house tomorrow?"

"The proofs are ready," Lissa confirmed. "Mrs. Craymore is anxious to see how they came out. To be honest, I'm looking forward to seeing their little girl again, too."

"She's a sweet thing," Aunt Enid agreed. "Maryanne has her father's fire and her mother's beauty."

After Lissa prepared for the night, she laid her Bible open on the bed in front of her. It was hard to concentrate. Her thoughts kept swinging to Brent and all Aunt Enid had told her about him.

Having come from a loving family, Lissa could not imagine what it must have been like for Brent to leave home and take his living into his own hands the way he did. A deep sense of respect came over her for him. It was no wonder he was the way he was.

Lissa's fingers smoothed the softened edges of the envelope she had used for a marker—the envelope with Knight's Inn's number. Dropping the edge of the envelope between the pages of her Bible, she shut it and reached to click off the bedstand light. Lissa sat silently in the darkness, listening to the sounds of the house ease into the night.

After a while, she slid off the side of her bed and walked over to the window. Lissa rattled the shade upward and stood looking across the yard at the darkened house where she knew Brent would be sleeping. Lissa prayed for him and wondered, with a sense of curiosity, at the impact Brent had had on her life over the past short weeks.

Lissa decided she liked Brent. She liked his somber seriousness...and the beginnings of the smile that teased the corners of his mouth during curious moments. She was grateful for the steps he was taking to renew his relationship with the Lord. She realized she also liked the blunt frankness with which he approached life.

And his eyes. Lissa especially liked his eyes. In all of her twenty-six years, she had never seen eyes with such depth or as unique as Brent's.

Smiling slightly, she turned and went to bed.

– 17 –

"Brent!" Maryanne cried happily as she raced down the front steps of her home. She flung herself at him and burst into giggles as he lifted her high and swung her around. "Brent, *stop* that!" she said and hugged him hard around the neck as he carried her on toward the house.

"Hello, Dallas," Lissa greeted Maryanne's shadow. The puppy flopped to his back and exposed his underside so Lissa could rake her fingers through his shiny red fur.

"Where's your daddy?" Brent asked.

"Out back talking with some other men. You know Daddy." Maryanne achieved a dramatic sigh and managed to get one hand on her hip. "The men are *always* talking...business, business, business."

Lissa permitted herself the bit of laughter that struggled to make itself heard. It was good to see the dancing light that appeared in Brent's eyes as he raised his brows with a sideward glance toward Lissa.

"Let me down, Brent." Maryanne pushed her small hands

against his chest. "Mommy said she'll see you in a minute, and I'm not supposed to bring Dallas in because he had another accident today. It wasn't anything expensive this time, but now Mommy says Dallas has to go to obedience school and I've been trying to teach him to behave a *little* before we take him to his class. I don't want his teacher to think he doesn't mind at all."

Maryanne raced down the porch with Dallas and vanished around the corner of the house.

"Maryanne is a darling," Lissa commented as she and Brent entered the Craymore home.

Brent nodded but did not reply. Lissa looked up at him. For some reason, and the suddenness of it surprised Lissa, the light was gone from his eyes.

With a lift of his hand, Brent waved the security personnel away. The two men Lissa saw melted back through the doors and disappeared, almost as if they had never been there.

In spite of the brightness and unexpected warmth of the day, Lissa felt a chill run down her spine. Again, she wondered what it must be like to live under the constant eye of other people. She did not like the feeling the thought gave her.

Olivia Craymore materialized from a side passage. The woman was as polished as she had been on Lissa's last visit, even in a pair of slacks and a simple blouse. As Lissa watched Olivia move toward her, she realized Olivia would be one of those people who would look beautiful no matter what she wore.

"You brought them?" Olivia asked. There was an aura of expectant excitement on her face. They moved to the sitting room and Lissa found herself seated on a richly brocaded sofa. The low table in front of her was accented by an arrangement of fresh flowers and the pleasing scent drifted around them.

Here," Lissa said, returning the smile Olivia gave as the

woman reached for the packet Lissa offered her.

"If you'll excuse me, I'll go find Walter." Brent exchanged glances with Olivia before allowing his gaze to linger on Lissa. "I won't be long."

"Don't worry about Lissa, Brent. We'll be fine. Oh," she exclaimed, holding up the first proof, "This is lovely."

As Olivia began to sift through the assortment of photographs, Lissa found her attention drifting toward Brent as he moved through an arched passage. The shadow of another man came up to him, and the two men bent their heads together as they walked on down the hall. Lissa heard the faint murmur of their voices echoing back to where she sat.

"He is handsome, isn't he?"

Lissa looked quickly back at Olivia. The expression on Olivia's face was serious. "Yes," Lissa agreed, "he is."

"You're good for him, you know. I've never seen Brent so taken with anyone before."

"What makes you say that?"

"Brent Jamison rarely sees a girl more than once. They don't put up with his...um...shall I say...overbearing attitude?"

"At the present, I believe ours is more what you'd call a working relationship."

"I know better. I know Brent." Olivia's hand rested briefly on Lissa's. "Deep inside he's got so much to give." She paused. "He's a good man."

The look in Olivia's eyes arrested Lissa. The beautiful eyes were soberly intense. Lissa stared back, not knowing what to say. The two of them were silent, then Olivia broke the spell and returned her attention to the photographs she had spread on the table.

Lissa watched Olivia as she began to chatter about first one, then another picture. Lissa answered a question or two,

111

but in the back of her mind she wondered about Brent...
about Olivia...about the relationship between the Craymore
and Jamison families. Disturbed curiosity went through Lissa.
What was it that held the friendships together?

– 18 –

With the coming of Thursday's pre-dawn hours, Lissa found herself awake and disturbed. A vague uneasiness filled her, and Lissa listened to the silent house.

She sat up in bed, her hand reaching out to turn on the light, but stopping instead to touch the Bible she had left open on the bedstand the night before. Her fingers touched the envelope. Paper against paper whispered under her touch.

What is it, Lord? What's going on?

The house creaked as it was prone to do now that fall was moving toward winter and the temperatures were dropping outside. Lissa pushed back her covers and stood upright. The room was chilly. Shadows flitted in the corners. Lissa made her way to the window and peered out at the darkness.

The guest house was lightless. Bony branches waved across the yard light, causing mysterious shadows to weave about the yard.

Lissa scanned the portion of the drive and garage that

113

was visible from the window. Something had caused her to awaken. Surveying the scene again, she saw the house, the trees, the garage....Lissa frowned, stepping quickly back from the window, but not so far that she could not see out. A shadow moved alongside the garage...on the far side from the guest house, and it was not unlike...the shadow of a man.

What would a man be doing sneaking around—?

Lissa stood rooted to the spot, watching as the form withdrew from the shadows long enough to....

Hanson!

Lissa's mouth went dry. He had come like he said.

Another thought riveted her to the floor: *How many other men would be after her?*

Lissa's fingers touched the key and ring dangling around her neck. *Lord, what is so important about this key?*

The guest house...there was no sign of Brent. Hanson disappeared. Lissa heard the barely existent creak of the kitchen screen door being opened.

Did Hanson have a key? Did he *need* one?

Spinning, Lissa tore off her night clothes and snatched at a heavy sweater and a pair of jeans that came to hand. Her trembling fingers could barely slip her tennis shoes on her feet. Racing into her clothes, she prayed.

Dear Father...you're going to have to show me what to do.

Lissa's heart pounded as she hurriedly locked the bedroom door. She drew a ragged breath.

The bed...the closet...there was no place to hide!

Lissa saw the window and rushed toward it. Her hands shook as she attempted to twist the lock. The short section of roof outside the window slanted gradually. From the edge it was a ten foot drop. She tried to remember a trellis or downspout, but could not. Surely there would be one at the corner.

114

Lissa stopped as she heard the middle stair give an insistent squeak. Aunt Enid's voice...inquiring. No reply. Aunt Enid again. There was a stringent tone to her words...and Aunt Enid suddenly went silent.

Fear for the older woman shot an additional shaft of horror through Lissa. The lock gave way. The window came open. She fought with the storm window and in her haste kicked out the remaining screen.

The doorknob rattled. Lissa thrust her body through the opening, very nearly slipping as her feet struck the slanted, shingled roof. An explosion of sound burst behind her. She dove for the corner of the roof, her scream sharply bitten off as she fought to keep from flying over the edge. Lissa stopped within inches of the gutter.

The darkened height spun dizzily before her eyes. Below were bushes. Not stopping to think of the consequences, Lissa rolled onto her stomach and dangled her legs over the edge. Her fingers tightened on the gutter—it groaned. She dropped to hang for one desperate second before she released her hold.

Lissa landed—more on her back than on her feet. The bushes dipped and swayed with her impact, springing back, protesting her weight. Momentarily dazed, she panted for breath, and attempted to right her swirling thoughts. Then she was up, fighting the bushes that now threatened to delay her escape. She sprinted across the lawn.

The guest house door was locked.

"Brent!" Lissa tried to keep her voice low so Hanson would not hear her.

Lissa tugged the doorknob, trying to twist it free.

"Brent!" Her fist connected with the framing. "He's after me! *Brent!*"

"Help me!" she cried. "Please, Brent...Hanson is after me!"

The door snapped back and Lissa fell through the dark

doorway. Brent thrust his car keys at her. "Go through the back door," he ordered.

"What about you?"

"I can't afford to expose my position yet. *There's too much at stake*," he emphasized when she would have protested. "Here," he lifted a large vase from a table in the entry. "Hit me."

"*What?*"

The look of exasperation that crossed his features had Lissa snatching the vase from Brent's hands. She hesitated, then, gritting her teeth, she drew back and swung.

The vase shattered against a suddenly lifted fist and Brent dropped backward in a dramatic, sprawled heap. Leaping over him, Lissa ran, searching for a back exit. She found one in the kitchen.

Cold snatched at her clothes as she shot through the door. Stopping at the corner of the back patio, Lissa peered cautiously around. She saw the utility entrance to the garage. Between was a tree and two empty flowerbeds. She heard the back door to the main house snap shut. Taking a series of deep breaths, Lissa counted to five, hoping Hanson would have made it to the front door of the guest house. She plunged forward, paused behind the tree long enough to take a hasty cursory glance around, and shot on to the garage.

The door was unlocked, and she hit the automatic opener button the moment she swung through.

Her fingers shook so hard she could barely insert the key in the ignition. The engine roared to life. Lissa slammed the gear shift into reverse and floored the gas pedal, the tires screaming as they arced a partial circle in the drive.

Appearing from around the edge of the screening bushes, Hanson sprinted for the car. Lissa caught sight of him from the corner of her eye as she struggled to put the car into drive. The yard light flashed on the gun he carried. His body dove for the car. Lissa hit the gas.

116

Hanson tumbled and rolled, the force of the racing car bouncing him away from the squealing tires.

Unfamiliar with the street layout and fearful of cornering herself in a dead-end, Lissa took the most direct route out of the housing area. Once on the main street and certain of where she was, she took a handful of abrupt turns, deliberately schooling herself to maneuvering tactics rather than speed.

Not that she slowed down. Grim concentration had her maintaining as fast a speed as she dared.

Headlights bobbed behind her. Taking another sudden turn, Lissa changed directions once more.

Where should she go?

She turned a corner, then turned again, decision made. Home.

– 19 –

Nestled in a collection of pine and silver maples, the McIntyre family home was a white two-story farmhouse with an attic. The sun had risen by the time Lissa drove up the gravel driveway. No one would be home, she knew. Her parents wintered in Florida, and Randy, the only son left at the family home, had remained in Colorado on an extended vacation with Darrell, another of her older brothers.

The sound of the car door closing reverberated against the backdrop of trees and into the icy air. Lissa trotted a path through fallen leaves to mount the steps to the front porch.

The house had a quiet feeling about it. Other than a faint suggestion of a breeze and a scolding from a blue jay somewhere in a tree behind her, Lissa heard no other sounds. The house was a quarter mile off the main road. Distance and the surrounding trees insulated the home from traffic noise.

The first thing she needed to do was to see if she could

get word to Brent. She did not know if he could find her here, and she admitted to herself—and God—that she was afraid.

After letting herself in, Lissa passed through the house to the kitchen where she looked up and dialed first Brent's number, then Aunt Enid's. When neither answered Lissa tried to calm the fear that welled up within her.

Restless fingers tapped the kitchen counter top, then shoved themselves inside the pockets of her jeans. Lissa hunched her shoulders as her glance flickered around the room.

What was she going to do now? Waiting gnawed at her already frazzled nerves. The passing weeks had lulled her senses to complacency, but now....

Lissa began to pace, then wander. She made her way back to the front staircase and up to her old bedroom. Out the window Lissa could see beyond the treehouse to the now barren orchard and over the series of short rolling hills that separated Karl's family home from the McIntyres'.

Oh, Karl...what a childish game has done to our lives.... Resistance.

A blast of cold air tumbled over Lissa when she swung the attic door open. Before mounting the stairs, she reached for the light switch. Another switch started the electric heaters running. Her darkroom was primitive and small, tucked under a slanted corner, but adequate—an addition to the house when Lissa turned twelve.

Lissa's lips twisted. Who would have thought the hours of companionship she and Karl spent up here would culminate in this?

Lissa sank onto one of a pair of stools monopolizing the floor space of the tiny darkroom. She swiped a hand across the enlarger cover. Dusty, but not bad. Scanning the shelves, Lissa noted there were still adequate chemicals for processing black and white.

Along the one wall bare of shelving hung a montage of assorted pictures. She stood and examined the memories, remembering the times spent growing up, playing, changing.

Lissa sighed. This room, although unchanged itself, had witnessed many transformations. Her focus was drawn back to the extra stool. How many times had Karl sat there? Lissa's hand crept of its own volition to the chain at her neck. Here, Karl had given her this ring, shared secrets, talked, and told her of his desire to become a photojournalist. When the time came, Karl also told her of his need for the Savior she already knew.

They had prayed together...Karl in his desire for forgiveness for his sins, Lissa in grateful thanks and encouragement. It had been a special time.

Now?...

Lissa flipped off the light switch. The old wooden steps creaked as she made her way down to the second level...and stopped.

"No!" Lissa cried. Her legs went strangely weak.

Hanson smiled...a smile that touched the edges of his lips and lifted slowly as a gleam of delighted evil in his eyes intensified. His tall, broad body filled the hall as he moved forward, closer. For a man so big, he moved horribly easily, almost gracefully...which sent shudders of distressed anticipation coursing down Lissa's spine.

Lissa backed away. She half crouched, preparing to run....Where? There was no place to go. Lissa had trapped herself in a dead end. There was no place to run!

Hanson drew closer and spied the exposed key around her neck. "I'll take that," he said.

"How did you find me?"

"I followed you. The key. Now." His voice did not raise, but the intensity of the look in his eyes had Lissa fumbling with the clasp.

"I don't know what it's for."

"Makes no difference." He took the chain Lissa held out and paused to study her. "I see why Jamison protected you so long." The look in his cold gray eyes made her skin crawl. "You're a pretty lady."

"Brent is...not that way."

Hanson threw back his head and roared with laughter. Lissa jerked at the sudden change. "I see he's got you convinced." He snatched Lissa's wrist in a quick movement, and Lissa bit back the cry of pain that struggled to be heard. Hanson's face was inches from her own and the laughter that had been on his features only seconds before was replaced with an expression so intense Lissa quavered before it.

"Your detective is as crooked as they come," Hanson hissed.

"Are...are you going to k-kill me?"

"Not yet." The big man eased back, retaining his grip while he dragged Lissa down the hallway toward the stairs.

"But...you will."

The smile the man gave was malicious. "Probably...unless Jamison decides to do it himself." Pulling open the front door, Hanson stopped. "That *is* what he does...or hadn't he told you?"

Dumbly, Lissa stared, open-mouthed.

Hanson began to chuckle. "I thought not."

"*No!*" Lissa denied. Hanson chortled with glee.

Cold air blasted Lissa while she trotted after Hanson to where he parked his car. But Lissa barely noticed.

It was not possible that Brent was a hit man. If anyone fit her picture of a hit man, it was Hanson...and his cruelty was emphasized by his desire to play with her mind, to cause doubts and torment her.

"Get in."

She did and began to pray...against the doubts...for protection...guidance...knowledge to know what to do.

Whenever they slowed, Lissa watched for a chance to

escape, but since putting the car into gear at the house, Hanson had taken hold of Lissa's wrist in a grip that she knew he would not release.

Familiar with the area they were driving through, Lissa grew suspicious when Hanson eventually skirted south of the city and swung beyond the southwestern corner. The longer they drove, the more curious Lissa became about their destination. When Hanson made a turn off the main road she realized the route was identical to....

It couldn't be! Attempting to reject the idea that came to mind, Lissa soon realized their destination was also familiar to her.

Incredulous, Lissa realized Hanson was driving her directly to...to Senator Craymore's home!

At Hanson's nod they were waved on by the security guards at the gate.

"Don't get any ideas," Hanson warned when he released Lissa's arm to put the car into park. "You're a long way from anywhere."

Lissa's heart pounded a slow, intense tempo. Attempting to lick the dryness from her lips, her mind whirled with the impact of the reality assaulting her.

Lissa scanned the yard for an escape route. Other than scrawny, newly planted trees, the lawn was clear for a hundred yards around the house. There was no place she could run for concealment—no way to dodge and hide...even if Hanson did let go long enough for her to run.

Several cars were parked in the circle drive, but the house was conspicuously devoid of servants and men hiding in secluded corners. Hanson forced Lissa up the stairs and then right to the lower balcony. They walked along a hall until Hanson knocked at a closed door. Opening the door, he jerked Lissa inside.

A scattered group of men...including the senator...faced her. One man occupied an upholstered chair in the corner.

A stack of papers was balanced on his knees. A tablet on which he had been writing notes had found a place on the floor beside him.

An older man Lissa had never seen stood beside the senator, listening and looking out a series of high, narrow windows. A view of the forested countryside could be seen through the panes of glass. Four others, one she recognized as another government leader, were at various places around the room.

Senator Craymore turned, his conversation stopping as he saw Lissa. The smile that evolved was slow and exacting in formation, but cold. Any thoughts Lissa may have had that this was all a mistake were completely dissolved.

"Miss McIntyre," the senator commented. "I trust you have finally provided the answers we have been waiting for."

"I don't know what you are talking about." She was surprised at how strong her voice sounded.

Hanson left Lissa standing a number of steps to the side of the door and strode across the room to hand the key and chain to Senator Craymore.

"Don't even consider it," the man in the chair said over the top of his glasses when Lissa's glance strayed to the doorway she had just entered. His voice was calmly dispassionate. He returned to his work, saying, "You wouldn't make it ten feet."

"Explain this to me," the senator said. Tinkling together, the key and ring glittered in the light from the window.

Looking around her, Lissa experienced the unnatural quiet of the room. The man in the chair straightened a sheet of paper on the pile. It whispered. The man next to the senator slid his hand into his pocket. Change clinked as coins slid against one another. Another man, seated on a sofa, lazily spun the ice in his drink.

"The chain and ring are mine. I have no idea what the key is for."

"I am correct in assuming it belongs to Mr. Karello." The statement was more question than comment.

"It was given to me to keep...and that's what I've done."

With a quick movement, the dangling objects landed in the senator's palm. "Be cooperative, Miss McIntyre. We can become persuasive if the need arises."

"I can't help you because I don't know anything."

"Let me assist in jogging your memory," Hanson said, sauntering toward her. Taking hold of a loose curl of her hair, he inspected it before looking at her with taunting gray eyes.

"Back off, Hanson." Again, the man in the chair. Hanson's mouth twisted distastefully, but he dropped the piece of hair he held. Lissa quickly brushed her hair back over her shoulders and avoided the look in Hanson's eyes.

A that moment someone knocked on the door. Lissa's heart surged with hope. The door swung open. Olivia Craymore walked into the room and immediately spied her husband.

"Olivia," the senator's attitude changed with a genuine smile. Walking quickly across the room, he deposited the chain with the ring and key into his pocket.

Lissa drew a hasty breath that went to a sudden gasp as she felt the prick of a sharp object touch a point in the small of her back. Hanson took a position slightly behind Lissa. The pressure of the knife tip was a warning—not painful, but direct and insistent.

"I hope I'm not disrupting your meeting," Olivia said to her husband, "but Maryanne fell ill on the way to Mother's, so we turned around and came back. I know this will put a crimp in your bachelor weekend, but I really couldn't take Maryanne on to Mother's if she is ill."

"Of course not," the senator agreed. A meaningful, cursory glance flashed over the people in the room. "If you will excuse me, I'll only be a moment. I would like to look in

124

on my daughter and make certain there is nothing seriously wrong."

At that moment, Olivia turned enough to see Lissa and her face lit up with surprise. "Lissa...what are you doing here? Darling," she faced her husband, "I thought this was only for you men." She paused. "Where is Brent?"

"It was my suggestion." This was from the man on the sofa. His ice tinkled in his swirling drink. "We heard about the excellent job Miss McIntyre did for you. A few of us had considered having portraits taken. Walter surprised us by having all of us meet her."

There was muttered agreement from two other men.

Olivia's gaze swung back to Lissa. "Is that true? How wonderful for you. I'm so glad Walter is passing the word. I did tell you, didn't I, that I'm mentioning to all my friends the excellent work you've done?"

The spot on Lissa's back pressured a sharp warning. She felt sick.

"Yes," Lissa replied, realizing her voice quavered more than was acceptable to Hanson or the senator. "This was...a complete surprise to me."

The senator spoke. "Olivia, I would like to see Maryanne."

"Of course, dear." Before the woman turned toward the door, she addressed Lissa. "When I've got Maryanne settled perhaps we could get some refreshments in the kitchen. I must tell you about the comments my friends have been giving me."

Lissa merely nodded, unable to utter the words of despair flowing to her mouth.

As the couple left the room, Lissa could hear Olivia saying, "I hope you don't mind, dear...I've called Mrs. Timothy to come ba...." Her voice disappeared as the door cut off sound.

"Very good," Hanson drawled behind Lissa. His breath tickled her ear. Lissa flinched. Her frightened look jumped from the man next to the window to the one on the sofa to the man in the chair. None did more than return a dispassionate glance.

How do I get out of this, Lord?

Brent...where are you?

Hanson's hand crept from where it lay heavy on her shoulder to wrap around and under her chin. It covered the entire width of her throat...and Lissa trembled at the nearness and threat of strength in the man's touch.

"Lay off, Hanson," the man with the papers ordered. His voice remained an even, conversational tone. He shifted through the top couple sheets of papers, then bent to retrieve the pad on the floor and make notations. His glance shifted upward to lock on Hanson who had not relinquished his grip. Seconds passed. The hand loosened and dropped away.

Lissa's shaking hands flew to cover where Hanson's had been. She sidestepped quickly, chancing retribution to get away from the man's overwhelming presence.

No one moved.

They waited.

Several minutes passed.

From the depths of Lissa's mind came a verse she had memorized from Jeremiah.

They will fight against you but will not overcome you, for I am with you and will rescue you.

It was like a cry to battle.

Thank you, Lord.

Despite her fears, Lissa was nudged with confidence. Everything would right itself, but she would have to do her part. She would have to identify the men. Lissa's heart prayed while her mind went to work.

Hanson she could easily identify. The man with the papers was slender, youngish, with nondescript brown hair, and an emotionless expression. He must be important if Hanson obeyed his commands. The man's brown eyes lifted to meet her gaze. He returned to his work.

The person who had been at the windows with Senator Craymore turned and paced a few steps. He appeared unhurried. He was an older man, grayed, slightly overweight, and paunchy around the middle. As she watched, the man slid his hands into his pockets and shook a handful of change...a nervous habit, maybe. He had done that before. The sound of clinking coins was loud and emphasized by the rustling of more papers from the man in the chair.

There was a tap at the door, the slight sound loud in the silence.

Lissa's head jerked around. The door swung inward as a spear of fright shot through her.

"Brent!" Lissa cried.

– 20 –

Lissa's forward leap was stopped short by Hanson's vise-like grip on her arm. The cry of pain was inevitable.

Brent's voice was composed, but pointed. "There's no need to hurt her."

"Now...aren't you the one to be telling me what to do?" Hanson sneered.

The man with the papers interrupted the tension forming between Hanson and Brent. "Let her go."

"Quit telling me what to do!" Hanson snarled back. "I found her; she's mine!"

The man laid his hands on the papers and continued to watch Hanson. With an abrupt sound of disgust, Hanson released Lissa, his face twisting with irritation.

Racing into Brent's arms, Lissa received a cold welcome. Lissa was stunned. Arms stiff, Brent pushed her back, to the side, placing himself between Lissa and Hanson.

At that moment, the senator reentered the room. "Glad you're back," he said to Brent. "We were about to start the meeting without you." He indicated Lissa. "You realize we have serious business to consider."

"So I've noticed," Brent replied. His cold, gray look touched Lissa. "You know none of this was necessary—especially not now."

"Have you gone soft on a pretty face, Brent?" The senator paced across the room, then turned. "I've never known you to let anyone interfere with business."

"When the action is pointless I see no need for expending the energy. I've always stressed doing things in order, Walter. You'll agree that's why my success rate has been so high. Miss McIntyre has nothing more to offer us than we had before." He readdressed his comments to Hanson, "And if you hadn't been so eager to get your hands on her, we wouldn't be wasting our time. How do you propose to destroy the evidence now? With Karello barely alive, we won't get any answers from him. We have no knowledge of whether he was able to contact anyone else, and Miss McIntyre hadn't a clue to what Karello has gotten himself into."

"I don't believe it," Hanson insisted. "You all saw her. A few hours ago this woman supposedly hit Jamison over the head with a vase, trying to escape. But what do we see here? She throws herself at him! How does that smell to you? To me, it *stinks*." His finger came up to jab at Brent, "You know more than you're telling. You're not operating strictly for us, anymore."

"*Right*...." Sarcasm dripped from that single word. Lissa was dumbfounded at the transformation in Brent. "What have you got that you can pin on me? Care to fill us in on the details?" His hands lifted to include the room of men. "My record with this organization is sterling." He paused for emphasis, his eyes darkening as his gaze narrowed. "Can you make the same claim?"

"We will have to decide what to do with her." The man

129

on the sofa planted his drink on the table beside him, the dull thunk of glass striking wood putting a period on his words.

"Eliminate her," Hanson argued, daring Brent to disagree.

"Not yet." Senator Craymore dismissed the thought with a lift of his hand.

A man, tall and hawkish, standing by the fireplace, said, "It will have to be done eventually."

Lissa cried, "What kind of people are you?"

The man in the chair smoothed the pile of paper on his knee and said, "Businessmen." The single, innocent word had an ominous overtone.

Lissa's glance touched the men in the room, coming to rest on Brent. She endured growing dread as she watched him play his part. He was good. So good...she wondered now where he really stood.

The senator agreed with the tall man, but said, "Let's not be hasty. Miss McIntyre can still prove to be a valuable tool. In the meantime...we have business to conduct. Hanson...." Cold fear overtook Lissa as the man's eyes gleamed with anticipation. She could not stop herself. She snatched at the fabric of Brent's jacket. "Take Miss McIntyre to your quarters and secure her for now. Our meeting's been interrupted long enough."

"I don't trust him, Walter." Brent twitched his arm, showing where Lissa was crushing the material. Lissa's heart pounded in her throat. She prayed the men would listen to Brent. "Mind if I go along to observe?"

"Hanson is capable of handling Miss McIntyre."

"Capable," said the paunchy man, "but he would do with some monitoring, I think. Remember what he did to the last person we had him secure?"

Lissa stared at the man in complete disbelief. How could this be happening to her?

"Go on," the person in the chair said, tipping his head in

the general direction of Brent's presence. "As late as it is, it won't hurt if we wait a little longer." He scribbled on the tablet, ignoring the rest of the men once his decision was made.

Hanson's face was sour but not defeated. A chill went through Lissa at the look shining in his eyes. He would kill her the instant he had the chance.

Brent disengaged Lissa's grip and grabbed her upper arm, leading her to the hallway.

Heart pounding, Lissa cried out silently in prayer—for her safety, for Brent's—she glanced quickly at his stony face looking for some form of encouragement, then at Hanson whose plans created an evil delight in his eyes.

Lissa prayed for all the men in that room, and the family elsewhere under the roof of this home bought by the...by the lives of...who knew how many other people?

Brent directed her down a branch hallway. They descended a short set of stairs. This was the servants' wing—a section she had not seen.

But what was going on? she wondered. Was all of this...for the glory of a handful of men and the gain of some prestige...power...money? It was so stupid, so senseless.

Doorways passed by. Hanson, from behind, taunted the two of them, warning Brent, threatening them both.

As she endured Hanson's continued baited remarks, Lissa became fervently aware that she was glad she was a Christian. She was glad she had lived her life before the Lord. She knew she wasn't perfect. But at least she had tried to live her life the way she believed Jesus Christ would have her do.

"In there," Hanson said, indicating a doorway on the left. Lissa slipped through, followed closely by Brent. Hanson clicked the door shut.

The room was a living area with a small kitchenette. Off to one side was a bedroom. The furnishings were simple, basic, with a sofa, an easy chair, a desk, and some chairs around a small table.

At Hanson's directive, Lissa pulled a chair away from the table and sat down, putting her arms behind the back of the chair. Her ankles were crossed and tucked back under the seat. Brent stood to the side, hands sliding into his pockets as he watched. "Not too tight," he ordered when Hanson began to twist a length of rope around Lissa's wrists. Her feet were already secure on the back rung. Vindictively, Hanson gave a jerk on the cords and Lissa cried out.

"I said," Brent's hand came down firmly on Hanson's shoulder, "not too tight."

Hanson's features darkened and he shrugged off Brent's grip. "Keep your hands off me, Jamison. No one tells me how to do my job. Not even you."

"We'll discuss that later...and how you dared to enter my home and strike my aunt. In case you don't realize it, your time is limited with this organization."

A bark of laughter, short-lived and sharp, came from Hanson. "We'll see about that. Could be you're the one ready to leave."

"Either way, I will loosen her bonds. The men won't stand for your cruelty this time."

Surprisingly, Hanson stepped back, but not without a tone of nastiness.

Brent adjusted the ropes around her wrists, picking at the cords to loosen them, but not as much as Lissa would have thought...until she felt Brent slip a small object into the palm of her hand. She quickly dropped her gaze to her lap so Hanson would not see the surprised look on her face.

"H-How long will you leave me here?" Lissa asked when the men turned to go.

"Maybe a couple hours. Probably longer," was Brent's reply. "I'll be back."

"We'll be back." Hanson grinned. "Be grateful for every

minute you have remaining." His cackling laughter mingled with the solid finality of the door being shut.

There was silence.

The sides of the chair cut into the soft flesh of Lissa's forearms, producing discomfort that competed with the ache in her hands. Her fingers were beginning to swell in spite of Brent's attempts. Lissa felt the tiny object and realized Brent had slipped her a small knife. Fumbling with the knife she found she was able to open the blade...only to have it slip from her grasp and drop to the floor!

No! What did she do?

In desperation, Lissa tried to pick at the knots, but found they were too tight. Her fingers could not grip the twisted cords with enough force to do any good. Tingling shots of electricity ran down the lengths of her fingers.

Cramps started in her shoulders, and Lissa whimpered as she tried to relax the muscles and ease the knotting pain. Her ankles ached.

There must be something she could do.

Concentrate.

On the floor...so close...was the knife, it's shining sliver of blade waiting...if she could only reach it.

Determined, Lissa threw her weight to the side. The legs of the chair barely lifted. She tried again, starting a rocking motion, adding greater height with each thrust until...the chair toppled sideways.

Pain...in her shoulder, her hip. Gritting her teeth, Lissa waited for the stabbing to ease There would be a horrible bruise. Her fingers tingled, the numbness growing.

Trying to see the knife, Lissa twisted her head around. Behind her.

She labored to move, twisting the chair and feeling, reaching with her fingers.

She could not...reach...it.

Trying to get a grip, Lissa struggled to retain the sensation

133

of feeling she knew she would need if she were going to be able to use the knife. But...hard as she tried, her fingers would not come close enough to grip the instrument.

Lissa lay on the floor, her cheek resting against the carpet, her fingers steadily losing feeling.

Determined, Lissa tried to roll to her back, pushing and rocking as hard as she was able, her fingers moving, reaching, touching....

She had it!

But the triumph was short lived. She could not maneuver the small blade with any accuracy. She tried again...and lost the blade.

Resentment grew in the pit of Lissa's stomach, and she did not try to stop the tears that formed.

What are you doing, Brent? Why did you leave me here? Why couldn't you have taken me with you?

The room was oppressively quiet. Minutes elapsed. Pain...in her arms, her hip.

"Lord, how could you allow this? Why?" Tears trickled paths across her face. Her arms and thigh throbbed in deep surges of pain. "Why couldn't you have helped me hold the knife? How can I stand this? What do you *want* from me?"

Trust.

Lissa's crying stopped abruptly. Holding completely still, she listened...but there was no sound.

Haltingly, Lissa dared to whisper, "What?"

Am I not able to take care of you?

The still, quiet voice struck her heart. Several seconds passed. Lissa closed her eyes in shame. "Yes, Lord." She sniffed, brushing the side of her face against the carpet to swipe away the traces of tears. "I'm sorry. What you don't need from me is a pity party." Lissa tried to relax. With the stillness of her heart, the pain in her body diminished.

Time passed. There was no clock. Lissa judged the hour by thin rays of sun from a shuttered window creeping along the wall. In turn, she prayed, then considered how she might escape, and wondered why no one came back. Ultimately, she dozed, sometimes coming to reality with a start when another cramp tore at her body.

It was getting late. The light faded. The carpet cut into her face. Lissa shifted her head so her hair cushioned her cheek.

Suddenly, a noise caught her attention. Lissa's head jerked up sharply. She hissed at the pain in her shoulders, grateful her hands had long since grown numb.

There was the sound again.

The door...Lissa watched the doorknob twist around.

– 21 –

The color drained from Lissa's face. This was it. The time was now.

The door swung inward.

Lissa's mouth dropped open.

The disturbed, astonished face of Olivia Craymore stared back!

The senator's wife let out a tiny cry of disbelief. She moved through the opened doorway and leaned back against the door.

"I didn't want to believe it could be true." Pained denial etched itself into Olivia's face. "Surely there's a...a reason...for...." She cried out in agony. "Not my husband. Not Walter! He's always been so good to me."

"Mrs. Craymore...please. Can you untie me?" Lissa spoke. "I need to get out of here."

Olivia did not seem to hear Lissa; she rambled, "I knew you couldn't be here for any good reason. Walter never invites someone like you to one of his meetings." She moved forward, hesitant, shocked. "That's what made me so suspicious. I mean, there have been other happenings, but you...you looked so frightened...and there was nothing I could do for you."

"Olivia," Lissa said carefully. "There is something you can do for me now."

Olivia's eyes focused with abrupt comprehension. "Yes. I can untie you." The words came out as if to reinforce what she had to do. She dropped to her knees beside Lissa. "I can do that. Yes, I can do that." She gasped in horror. "Your *hands*."

"At least I'm still breathing, Mrs. Craymore."

The denial that crossed Olivia's face was pathetic. "You can't mean...." Tears began to shine in the distraught woman's eyes. "But...."

The woman struggled to make some good out of her husband's evil. Her fingers slipped from the knots that bound Lissa's hands. She cried, frustrated. "I can't do it. The knots are too tight."

"The knife," Lissa suggested. "There on the floor. I dropped it—couldn't use it."

Olivia's fingers coiled around the knife. She worked, jabbing, gnawing, managing as carefully, but as quickly as possible, to secure the tip of the knife under one of the wrappings of rope. Olivia chipped away at each separate strand until the cords frayed and popped loose.

Lissa had not expected the pain that happened along with the sudden rush of blood that flowed through her fingers. Her hands were an awful sight, swollen and purpled, useless. Her arms were wracked with pain and were barely movable. Her loosened legs felt the fire of reawakening nerves.

"Is the...senator still here?" Lissa gritted.

Olivia gently tried to massage away the distress Lissa suffered. "They're gone," she said. "All of them are gone. I don't know where to. Business, I was told. I saw Hanson leave...all of them leave...without you. I knew you hadn't left," Olivia said. "I just...had to find you." She helped Lissa to her feet. Lissa swayed, her legs protesting.

"Do you know what's going on?" Lissa asked.

Olivia looked ill. She shook her head. "I've suspected, but...."

"It's not safe for you to stay here," Lissa told her. "Not since you've freed me. These men are coldly methodical about the way they work."

"But Walter is...my husband." The words were almost a whimper.

"I'm certain the police can provide safe housing."

"He would never hurt me."

"There are others who would."

Torn, the woman fought within herself. "I couldn't...leave him," she said. "Maryanne...what would she think? What would I tell her? How could I...?"

Olivia stared helplessly at Lissa.

"I'll help you get Maryanne ready," Lissa offered. She looked at her hands. She could move the fingers now. "But we should hurry."

Lissa waited an eternity of seconds as Olivia considered her choices. Painfully resolved, the senator's wife nodded stiffly, agreeing.

It did not take long for Olivia to pack several cases. Maryanne was sick, but not so ill that she could not travel. As long as Dallas went along, Maryanne considered the experience a great adventure, and Olivia chose not to dissuade her daughter otherwise.

In the end, Olivia Craymore decided to go to her mother's home. She agreed that police protection was probably best, but could not bring herself to believe that her husband would allow anyone to harm her or their daughter.

At Lissa's request, Olivia dropped Lissa off at police headquarters downtown. Lissa watched with some misgiving when Olivia Craymore's car drove away from the police station. It was dark. Lissa shivered in the cold. The taillights of Olivia's car vanished in the moving traffic.

Lissa wondered if the woman was going to be all right. The drive to town had passed in silence. It was obvious Olivia was suffering.

She would have to be strong. Any politician meddling in controversial—criminal— affairs...well, Lissa suspected that when this all became public, the Craymore family would be crucified by the press.

Feeling sorry for Olivia, Lissa turned and prayed that the senator's wife would have the strength she would need to make the right decisions about her husband, Maryanne, and herself.

Walking inside the police station, Lissa had no idea what being placed under protective custody would entail, but she was in no mood to turn her back on the thought. Having been close to death and, she was certain, divinely rescued, Lissa did not plan to take any more chances.

Besides, she was tired...and sore. Her entire body hurt. Although her hands were improving, she suspected it would take a number of days before they were back to normal. She wanted to think she could trust Brent's co-workers enough to keep her safe so she could at least get some rest.

Food wouldn't be bad, either. She could not remember the last time she had eaten, and her stomach was letting her know that she should do something about another meal.

Lissa's mind flitted between these different thoughts, interspersed with disturbing recollections from the previous twenty-four hours. She prayed again for the situation she found herself in, and added prayer for Karl, Brent, and Olivia Craymore. The people instigating all this evil were not forgotten, either. God was as able to change their lives as He was able to protect others.

In spite of the late hour, police headquarters was a busy

139

place. Within seconds of identifying herself and mentioning Detective Bendar's name, Lissa was ushered down a hall and up an elevator. Lissa's stomach gave a lurch as the elevator stopped. Halls branched off in all directions. Within three quick turns, Lissa was lost.

Lissa and her escort passed through two doors, and with each passing they met fewer people, until they were in a portion of the building specifically set aside for special task forces.

Detective Bendar was a short, stocky man with bright blue eyes—nothing Lissa would have expected him to be. But what did she expect anymore? Only the unexpected, she thought as a wry twist crossed her face. She brushed her hair back from her face with a weary hand.

The last door they passed through led into a smaller, comfortable room containing a desk, several chairs, and a long sofa. Detective Bendar disappeared through another door off to the side and reappeared in a few moments carrying a pillow and neatly folded blanket.

"I have to tend to a couple items," he said. "You'll be fine here until arrangements can be made for you to be placed in a safe house. I thought you might like to lie down," he added. "You look dead on your feet."

"At least I only look it. Sorry," she said a second later, grimacing. "Bad joke. I am tired," she agreed. "I'm hungry, too."

"I'll find some food."

"When will I see Brent?"

"I'm not certain," the detective replied. "He hasn't checked in for hours. We expected you before now," he added.

"How long will you be gone?" Lissa asked as the detective turned to leave the room.

"A few minutes. Relax until I come back."

Once Detective Bendar left the room, locking the door behind him as a precautionary measure, Lissa turned to the

140

sofa where the detective had laid the pillow and blanket. She grabbed the pillow by a corner and pulled it up against the arm of the sofa. It looked comfortable—not one of the skinny, flat kind, but a soft, plump cushion.

Lissa gave in and sank onto the sofa, nuzzling the side of her cheek into the cool pillowcase. She was so tired. Her body ached with pain and the stress of the past many hours. Inspecting her hands through half-closed eyes, she saw the puffiness was leaving. They still hurt, though, and there was bruising around her wrists.

She wondered where Brent was and what he was doing.

Her eyes shut. A tiny sigh escaped her lips. If Detective Bendar did not hurry with the food, she was afraid she would be asleep before he got back.

A set of keys rattled at the door. Lissa heard the lock snick back. Heavy eyelids forced themselves open to watch the door swing inward.

Frowning, Lissa shoved herself upright and asked, "Who are you?"

– 22 –

The man standing in the open doorway was dressed in a trim, three-piece suit. He was clean shaven with light brown hair neatly combed. His face was pleasant, but Lissa watched him closely.

"Miss McIntyre?" the man asked.

Her head buzzed with fatigue. "Who wants to know?"

"I'm Marvin Frost, FBI. I'm here to conduct you to a safe house. If you'll come with me?"

"Where's Detective Bendar? He said he'd be right back."

"He's been detained. We must hurry. The quicker we act the less chance we have of anyone discovering your whereabouts."

Lissa studied him, not saying anything. "Detective Bendar said he would be back in a few minutes. I'd prefer to wait until he arrives."

"Fine." Mr. Frost crossed his arms and leaned back against the doorjamb, preparing to be patient. "I understand your hesitation, but you may be in for a long wait. His superiors got hold of him, and they'll have him trapped in the conference room for an hour or two."

Lissa eyed the man dubiously.

"He said you'd be hungry," Mr. Frost added. "I'm supposed to feed you on the way."

Lissa wavered. "Where are you planning to take me?"

"If everyone knew your destination, Miss McIntyre, then it would no longer be a safe house."

"But I'm the one going there. I should at least be able to know where you're taking me. I have people to contact, a business to run. I can't just walk out and disappear."

"For the time being you have to do exactly that. We can't take any chances with your life. Your testimony in combination with the work that has been going on for the last eighteen months is going to crack this case wide open."

"How do you know how important or not important I am?"

Mr. Frost smiled tolerantly. "I've worked very closely with this case. Detective Jamison has been keeping our people informed of you and your efforts to help apprehend Senator Craymore and his associates."

"All I've been doing is trying to answer a few questions and stay alive."

"Then you understand the need to leave as quickly as possible."

"I would rather see Detective Bendar first," Lissa said.

"I understand, but I'm afraid that isn't possible."

"Couldn't we stop wherever he's at so I can at least talk to him?"

His head shook. Sympathy crossed Mr. Frost's features. "I'm sorry, I have my orders." His hand came out, indicating the open doorway. "Shall we?"

Uneasily, Lissa watched this man. It seemed obvious Mr. Frost had been sent by Detective Bendar. How else would he have known she was hungry? And if Mr. Frost were really working closely with the case, he would probably know more about her than she did.

Brent had not said anything about the FBI being involved. But had he said much about the case at all?

"Let me see your identification," she said.

He complied, holding it out so she could inspect the photograph and information.

Lissa's mouth twisted to the side. She looked with regret at the dented spot on the pillow beside her. "Are you sure I can't see Detective Bendar?"

"He'll be in contact with you, that's all I can say."

"Has there been any news from Detective Jamison?"

"None."

The sigh that came from Lissa's lips was one of resignation. She stood up and followed Mr. Frost down the hallway. After a number of turns, Mr. Frost opened a door and indicated that Lissa was to enter the office ahead of him. The furnishings, Lissa noted, were modern, the room illuminated by a low light over the desk.

"You'll need a coat, first of all," Mr. Frost said, walking around the desk to open the middle drawer. "I see you haven't brought anything with you." He pulled out a thick file.

"All of this was rather sudden."

"We'll also need to have some information," his look flicked toward her, "but that can wait until later. I see food and rest is a priority here. Come," he lifted the file in the direction of the door as he retraced his steps back around the desk.

"Can I at least leave a note for Brent?"

The man appeared to think. "If you'd like." He laid the file on the desk, "But seriously, please make it short." A sheet of paper, removed from another drawer, rustled in his hand. He laid it alongside an envelope on top of the desk. "Every minute we stay can mean more danger for you."

"In a building full of policemen?"

"You'd be surprised, Miss McIntyre." Mr. Frost retrieved the file. "We are not impenetrable here. Some of the men we are dealing with are very powerful and ruthless."

Mr. Frost tactfully moved just outside the door. Lissa sank into a chair in front of the desk and pulled a pen from a small container standing to the side of the blotter. The remaining pens shifted, rattling against the metal side of the container.

What should she write?

Dear Brent,

What was it she wanted to say? Lissa shoved at her hair, and memories re-ran themselves in her mind.

I've been told I have to go with Mr. Frost. He won't tell me where we are going. I wish I had seen you or Detective Bendar first. Please come for me as soon as you can. I feel...uneasy about all this, but I do trust you. I'll be waiting.

She added, *You still haven't taken me out for a Greek dinner. I'm holding you to it. We have a lot to talk about,* and signed her name.

The paper crackled as she folded it into thirds and slid it into the envelope. She sealed the letter shut and added Brent's name to the outside.

What prompted her to do what she did next, she was not certain, but Lissa threw a quick glance over her shoulder to see Marvin Frost's outline against the opaque glass in the door. Working quickly, she leaned across the desk and withdrew another sheet of paper and envelope from the drawer. *I'm with Marvin Frost*, she wrote, adding *L Mc*. On the outside of the envelope, she once more wrote Brent's name. Folding the stuffed envelope in half, she barely had time to secure it under the waistband of her jeans and pull the sweater back into place before Mr. Frost rattled the doorknob and poked his head back into the room.

"Are you ready?" the man asked.

145

"Yes." Lissa snatched the first envelope and stood, turning to hold it out. "Will you deliver this?"

The envelope disappeared into an inside pocket of the man's suit jacket. "I'll see that it's taken care of," he assured her. Pointing, Mr. Frost indicated an elevator.

"I really need to make use of that room," Lissa moved toward a door with a silhouette of a woman on the front, "before I go anywhere."

Mr. Frost's patience seemed to be wearing thin. His lips thinned to a narrow line, then twisted upward in an accommodating smile. "I'll wait," he said.

Lissa pushed through the door and heard it whisper shut behind her. Looking hastily around she decided there was no one else in the room. She pulled the envelope from its hiding place, then stood it up, name plainly visible, on the narrow ledge below the mirror.

Just one person, the right person, was all she needed to see her letter and make certain it got to Brent. If Marvin Frost was who he said he was, it would make no difference. But if he wasn't....

Lissa could not shake the nagging feeling that something was wrong. For a moment she stood still. If she really suspected Mr. Frost, why go with him? Wouldn't it be safer to insist on staying right where Detective Bendar had left her?

The thing was, Mr. Frost had been agreeable with every protest she had given. If he was out to kidnap her....

Kidnap?

Lissa gave herself a small shake. What was she thinking? The whole idea seemed rather silly. Nevertheless, when Lissa walked from the room, the letter to Brent remained on the narrow shelf under the mirror.

The elevator took them to the garage level. On the way down, Mr. Frost stopped long enough to pick up a coat for Lissa. It was a man's coat, too big, but heavy and warm,

146

and Lissa did not complain.

The parking garage was drafty and cold with a low ceiling. Even if Mr. Frost had not suggested it for concealment's sake, Lissa would have pulled the hood over her head just to stay warm. Her breath was frosty. Fatigue and hunger were taking their toll, too, and Lissa began to shake.

The eerie, empty echo of their footsteps did not help Lissa's frame of mind. In spite of herself, she edged closer to Mr. Frost, her look shooting from one empty car to another.

Mr. Frost led her quickly to a parked sedan several spaces away. The rattle of his keys filled the room with sound as he unlocked the passenger door and helped Lissa into his car. She huddled in the seat, pulling the coat tighter around her as Mr. Frost entered the driver's side and slid under the wheel. He reached behind them to drop the file he carried on the back seat.

"How long will it take to get there?" Lissa asked. Her voice was whispery thin even to her own ears.

"Close to an hour. It's late, but if we can find a drive-up still open, we'll get something to eat. If not, there'll be something at the house. It's well stocked, so you won't starve, if nothing else."

Lissa nodded. She was having a hard time keeping her eyes open and her stomach churned with emptiness. Lissa wished she were home, warm, filled, sleeping in her own bed, preparing for another day of work at Created Images.

Would life ever be the same again?

Mr. Frost did find a place open. The hamburger he ordered helped fill the hollow in Lissa's midsection. While she was eating, Lissa cast a sideways study at Mr. Frost. She watched him steer and fold back the paper on his hamburger at the same time. His teeth clamped on the side of his sandwich.

Lissa took a sip of her coffee. The warmth flowed down to settle in her stomach. Despite her weariness, she was beginning to feel better now that she had eaten some food.

The miles passed in silence. The roads were nearly empty. Only an occasional glow of lights shone on the road ahead of them, then came closer and swept by, heading in the opposite direction.

The town they finally reached was small, silent, and sleeping for the night. Lissa struggled out of her half-drowsy state as Mr. Frost swung into a driveway, past a row of hedges and pines.

Except for one welcoming light shining in the back, the house was large, dark, and foreboding. Misgiving shook Lissa until Mr. Frost said, "I know it looks creepy, but inside it's really quite pleasant."

"Will you be staying, Mr. Frost?"

"I'm expected back at headquarters to report. A female police officer is already here, plus a man stationed for security. You'll be safe," he assured her. Lissa did not answer.

Inside, the female officer introduced herself as Gina Bergmann. Gina did not look like an officer in her jeans and oversized sweatshirt, but that was to be expected, Lissa supposed, since she assumed the people connected with the house were not to draw undue interest from the neighbors.

In her muddled state, Lissa mused over how the woman was playing Resistance and did not even know it.

"I've got a bed ready for you," Gina said.

Lissa muttered an unintelligent reply, vaguely realizing she made no sense. She heard Mr. Frost's voice from somewhere far away as she was led down a short hall into a bedroom. Gina was talking, but her words were meaningless.

Lissa felt the refreshing chill of a clean pillowcase against her cheek. Someone...Gina...tugged at her feet. The dull thud of her shoes dropping to the floor was the last thing Lissa remembered before she sank into blessed oblivion.

– 23 –

Tap, tap, tap....

Lissa frowned at the staccato regularity invading her dreams. She burrowed deeper under the warmth of her covers.

Tap, tap, tap, tap....

Threads of a pleasant memory, the dreamy vision already being forgotten as reason drifted toward reality, shifted further and further from her mind.

Tap, tap, tap...the sound forced its way unpleasantly into her brain.

Lissa groaned. She was so tired.

What was making that noise?

Tap, tap, tap, tap, tap....

Fingers curling themselves around the edges of her covers, Lissa drew them back from her face and squinted her eyes open sleepily....

Senator Craymore!

Lissa bolted upright in the bed, fully awake. He sat in a

chair, next to a table...just steps from her bed.

Lissa's muddled brain struggled to clear itself from the unthinkable. That this man should be here, was entirely... incredibly...out of place.

A lamp was on low. Shadows darkened the edges of the room.

Tap, tap, tap—a pen connected rhythmically against the table's glass top. The senator sat, legs crossed, expression observant. A file—papers and photographs shuffled—was spread under the tapping end of his pen.

Abruptly the sound halted. The senator's hand was still.

"You, Miss McIntyre," the senator said, sliding his pen back into his jacket pocket, "are one of the luckiest, most industrious people I have ever known."

Lissa stared at him, her heart thudding in her throat. She felt lightheaded.

"How did you escape?" the senator asked.

"You may as well give up," Lissa managed, her voice husky from sleep. "You're never going to have me eliminated." Where were Gina and the guard?

"Do not be so certain, Miss McIntyre. I have a friend in the hall who would love to prove you wrong."

Hanson? Brent? Or someone else?

The wrong assumption could get her killed.

Lissa asked, "What have you done with Gina?"

"The other woman that was here? Contrary to what you may believe concerning me, I do not deliberately set out to remove everyone in my path. It's only people who have become a liability that I seek to dispose of. The other woman is sleeping. Very soundly. I doubt that she will awaken before the day is well spent. By then you will be long gone." His voice became deceptively soft. "And I do mean gone."

Lissa attempted to steady the growing fear welling up in her. She clutched the blankets.

150

Did the senator know about the guard outside? How did the senator discover her hiding place? How was she going to escape? If the guard was still outside, he would have seen the senator and his henchman.

Okay, Lissa thought. No guard. Escape is up to me.

"What to you plan to do to me this time?" Lissa asked. "You realize, of course, that there's more to my preservation than luck. I have Someone very powerful watching over me."

"Detective Bendar is dead."

The words rang with finality.

Lissa knew she paled. *Bendar?* "How?" The word was hollow.

"Mr. Frost is efficient...especially when well paid. In fact, at this moment he's on his way to a sufficiently remote country to live out his life in modest luxury. I decided this was the last task he was to do for me."

Lissa stared at the senator. Marvin Frost: quiet, neat, courteous—traitor. Lissa forced her mind to work, to concentrate. "If Mr. Frost is one of your employees, why didn't he just take me to you in the first place?"

"Former employee," he corrected her. "Because it was easier for Mr. Frost to convince you to go to the safe house, then take the time to notify me. I thought it was rather diplomatic of him. It's much easier to remove a willing victim from one safe haven to another than one who is screaming or trembling with fear."

"You realize your wife knows what you are."

The senator uncrossed his legs and sat forward. He eyed Lissa suspiciously. "What are you talking about?"

"How else do you think I was able to escape? She's suspected you for quite some time."

"That is not true."

A sick, greenish-yellow color began to seep into the senator's face. His eyes darkened and the skin around them drew tight. Lissa could see a slight tremor that caused his hands to twitch as he grasped the arms of his chair.

Senator Craymore must truly love his wife, Lissa realized. For some reason that was a shock to her.

"I would never have gotten loose if it hadn't been for her," she continued. "Olivia knows about you. What she doesn't know she suspects. You won't find her home when you return tonight. After releasing me, she took Maryanne and left."

"You're lying."

Lissa shook her head. "Olivia dropped me off at police headquarters. How else do you think I was able to get there? I had no car, remember?"

"Get up," the senator said. His voice was even and the look in his eyes had changed to one of pure hate.

Lissa shifted the covers, never removing her gaze from the senator. Even as she watched he changed, his features etching themselves into a hard mask of revenge...and Lissa began to wonder at the impulsiveness with which she had spoken.

"Are we leaving?" she asked. Her coat lay over the back of another chair, not far from the senator. The senator's glare was poisonous. Lissa pushed her feet into her shoes on the floor beside the bed. "May I put on my coat?"

"Do that," came the clipped words.

The senator started to rise.

Lissa grasped the man's coat she had been given by the collar. The material was heavy, with sufficient weight to....

Lissa jerked the coat around with the force needed to slap the senator a resounding smack. His head jerked back. He tumbled into the chair, tangled in the billowing folds of material.

Lissa dodged the blindly outflung arms. A muffled roar escaped the covering. Lissa took a calculated risk and slapped the cover shut on the file. She had seen enough to realize

152

it was the file on the senator himself.

Uncovered, the senator flung himself from the chair with a shout. Lissa bolted, flinging another chair into his path.

The door burst open, but Lissa did not stop to look. She dashed into the bathroom and whirled, slamming the door shut. The lock snapped.

The house was an old one. The door was heavy. But Lissa knew neither the bolt nor the door was a match for someone like Hanson. And Hanson or some other henchman it would have to be. If Brent had been with the senator, he would have come in the bedroom at the same time as the senator.

The file...Lissa realized she had lost some material as she ran, but much was still there. It would need to be hidden. An outside yard light created an aura of weak blue light in the room. Lissa spied a cupboard.

The door behind her shuddered with a blow from the other side. Voices spewed angry words. Lissa jammed the file deep between a pile of towels at the back of the cupboard and shut the door. It was so obvious it might work.

Protesting groans came from the framework as once more a man threw his body against the door. Lissa could hear his malignant, grunted phrases.

Forcing the lock on the window, Lissa hissed. She had no time to consider the pain in her hands. A paper crunched under her feet. Too late to think of what she dropped. Crowding her body through the window, she jumped, dropping hard to her hands and knees.

Damp cold cut through her. Lissa sprang up. There was a commotion in the bushes to the side of the house. She spun and raced in the opposite direction.

Lissa's heart felt as if it were about to burst. Her breath came in labored panting. She did not know where she was going, but ran, ducking tree branches, shoving through hedges, scrambling over fences and racing down alleys.

A dog snarled and attacked a fence that bordered the second alley she cut into. The extra spurt of fear provoked by the angry barking forced her to take a sharp turn through another yard. Hesitating, she gave a quick glance up and down a vacant street, then sprinted across into the obscurity of another tree-lined yard.

This yard was different, she realized when her feet slapped onto the blacktop of a parking lot. From the dark outline of the building, Lissa knew she was in a church parking lot.

Her breath tore at her throat. She felt weak. Her mind spun and her thoughts became hazy.

Stumbling against the coarse brick wall of the building, Lissa threw out her hands to keep from falling. Sharp pain cut through the still swollen flesh. She gave a whimpering cry.

To her right...a door. She grasped the doorknob and the door swung open. Nearly tumbling, Lissa swung through. She paused, leaning up against the wall, trying to catch her breath.

Darkness. Moonlight filtered ghostly-colored shadows across the rows of pews stretching before her.

Think.

What she needed was a telephone. Lissa forced herself to move forward. Her breath rasped loudly in her ears, seeming to echo against the peaked roof of the sanctuary. She turned a corner, feeling her way, praying for an office door.

The first door was a small nursery. She could make out the outlines of a rocking chair and the edge of a crib. Lissa moved on. The next was a closet. The next a bathroom. Lissa stumbled through the hall, guilt pricking at the fringes of her insides. *Breaking and entering—that's what this is.* She had broken into a church!

Please.

Through another open doorway she spied a small desk. *A telephone!*

There was a moment of silence as she caught her breath. Her hand reached for the phone, her finger hit "0"...and she heard a whisper of sound outside the door just as a beam of light flashed on and sliced the air across the desk.

– 24 –

The shaft of light cut toward Lissa's outline framed against the window. Lissa trembled. Her mind envisioned an inky darkness splattered with the brilliance of a thousand stars.

"No!" she moaned. The telephone thumped back into its cradle, her numbed fingers unable to hold its weight. She sagged to her knees. The light in her eyes competed with the sparks that whirled through her consciousness. Her hands were heavy. She could barely raise them to shade her eyes from the glare. She struggled with her fading grasp of reality.

"Dear Lord Jesus, *please*," Lissa whimpered. "I can't run anymore. I haven't the strength. Set your angels around me to protect me." Lissa's voice trailed off with the last syllables. She slumped to the floor.

An overhead light turned on, flooding the room with a yellow glow. Lissa paid no attention. Her eyes were closed, her tangled hair covering her face.

With a detached sense of observance, Lissa felt hands on her...large hands...lifting, picking her up.

I tried, Lord. I really did try.

She was being moved. Outside. Cold emphasized the shaking that had begun to surge through her body. Lissa fought to push aside the darkness that threatened to hold her. Icy wind mingled with whirling stars. She tried to move, to resist, but her body refused to respond.

There was a firm surface against her back. The pressure of arms supporting her eased. Lissa shifted, able to drag her hands to her closed eyes. She pushed quaking fingertips across her face, flinching at the pain that shot through her palms. Piteous sounds came to her ears, and Lissa knew they came from her. She bit her lip to stop them.

Curling her hands to her chest, Lissa twisted, shoving her face into the upholstery of a creaky surface. Exhaustion and hurt pulsated through her body. She sucked in a shaky breath...and cried out when a hand grasped her shoulder.

"It's all right," a feminine voice said. "We may not be the angels of the Lord, but He may have sent us in their place."

Disbelieving the cadence of the voice, Lissa twisted her head. She squinted against the muted light of a lamp. A blanket was shaken and fluffed over her.

The woman, her long, dark hair framing her face, looked back as she tucked stray blanket corners around Lissa. Concern shadowed the woman's face, but it was kind. Then her blue eyes narrowed.

"Louis," the woman said, still watching Lissa. "Bring a damp cloth, too." Her cool fingers gently touched the side of Lissa's face, drawing the chin around closer to the light. "Those scratches could not have caused that much blood," she said, and gently pulled the covers back. Taking hold of Lissa's hands, she made a sound of dismay.

"Louis," the woman raised her voice over her shoulder, "please hurry with that cloth and warm water."

Lissa looked. Lacerations covered the palms of her hands.

Smears of dirt covered the scrapes, and brittle fragments of leaves clung to the drying wounds.

A man appeared through a doorway. Louis. He was tall and broad with a strong face. He gave Lissa a thoughtful look as he handed his wife a damp cloth. "I've got hot water on for tea, Katey," Louis said. He watched her cautiously dab blood and dirt away from the edges of the abrasions. Lissa hissed when a piece of gravel bit into the sore flesh.

"I'm sorry," the woman breathed. "I don't want to hurt you." Her gaze lingered on Lissa's face. "Do you want to tell us how it happened?"

Lissa drew a shuddering breath. She looked from the woman to Louis. "It's...difficult to explain."

"At this time of night," Katey said, "we'd believe almost anything." She touched the cloth to Lissa's hand, patting away what she could without causing more discomfort.

Louis asked, "What were you doing in my office?"

Lissa's stomach dropped with a sickening lurch. "You're the pastor of the church?"

"That's right," the man answered. "Pastor Louis Vander Lynden." His hand came to rest on the woman's shoulder. "This is my wife, Katey." Katey's blue gaze lifted to meet Lissa's.

Breaking and entering. The words sang in Lissa's head.

Lissa licked her lips. They were dry.

"The church door was unlocked," Lissa said. "I wasn't going to steal anything. Honest. I just needed to use the phone."

Louis and Katey exchanged a brief look.

Katey said, "If the door was unlocked, then you were supposed to get in. But what were you running from?" In response to the question that appeared on Lissa's face, she added, "We saw you cross the parking lot. We had just driven in from a trip out of state." The cloth lifted as she gestured. "This house borders the church grounds, and our driveway divides the two."

"I...." Lissa faltered, seeing the expectant faces before her. What was she supposed to say? What sort of plausible explanation could she give? She withdrew her hand from Katey's grip. "I need to make a phone call."

There was silence as the three people studied one another. Louis shrugged at the look from his wife. It was not that they disbelieved Lissa, but Lissa knew it was all so odd.

Pastor Louis cleared his throat. "May I make it for you?"

Lissa's head shook. "This is...complicated. It could be," she realized how tritely melodramatic she might sound, "dangerous. If...I...could just borrow the phone. It's long distance. I promise I'll pay you back."

Louis and his wife exchanged another glance. Louis waved aside Lissa's promise. "The telephone is in the kitchen." He reached for her. "Are you able to walk?" Katey's hands helped support Lissa's attempt to sit up.

"I can," Lissa assured them both with a confidence that wavered as she struggled upright.

Louis had a stack of local phonebooks and quickly found the one she needed. Lissa sank into a chair beside the couple's small kitchen table. She carefully tapped the series of numbers needed to connect her with Brent's police headquarters.

Katey moved about the room, pouring hot water into three cups and dropping tea bags in to steep. Pastor Louis leaned back against the short length of counter top to wait.

A number of rings buzzed in Lissa's ear. They cut off as a female voice greeted her.

"Detective Brent Jamison, please," Lissa stated firmly. "Or Detective Sidney Bendar." Lissa prayed the senator was mistaken about Detective Bendar. She felt rather than saw the relieved surprise on Louis and Katey's faces.

"One moment, please," the voice said in Lissa's ear. Lissa waited impatiently through a series of clicks. She pushed

159

her hair off her forehead with the back side of her forearm. The pain in her hands sent insistent messages of protest all the way to her shoulders. Another voice answered and identified himself. Lissa made the same request to speak to Brent.

There was a distinct pause. Lissa's heart dropped as the space in time lengthened. The man said, "Detectives Jamison and Bendar are...unavailable. How may I help you?"

"Is he...are they...all right? How can I reach Brent?"

The tone in her ear sharpened. "Is this Lissa McIntyre?"

"Where is Brent?"

"Where are *you*?"

"I need to talk to Brent." Lissa drew a breath. "I'm scared; I don't trust any of you, and I want to talk to Brent! If you don't tell me where he is in ten seconds or less, I'm hanging up!"

"It's all right, Lissa," the detective's voice spoke calmly and distinctly. "We'll get you in contact with Brent. In the meantime, I can have protection sent to you until he arrives. Where are you now?"

Lissa's teeth connected in frustration. She did not want their protection. She did not trust them. Only Brent or Detective Bendar.

"Miss McIntyre," the man said again, "where are you staying?"

Lissa hung up the phone.

Thinking quickly, Lissa grabbed the telephone book once more and shoved pages back, searching for Brent's home number. It was a possibility—one she could not afford to pass up. There was no answer from the guest house, so Lissa dialed the main house. The phone rang a number of short bleeps.

"Hello?" came a cautious, quiet voice.

"Aunt Enid?" Lissa asked.

"Lissa, is that you?"

160

"It's me. Where's Brent? Please, let me talk to him."

"I can't," Aunt Enid said. "He's not here. I haven't seen him. Did you try the station?" Lissa answered in the affirmative. "I can give you two other numbers to try…this one," Aunt Enid quoted a string of numbers that Lissa painfully scribbled onto a small pad Katey placed in front of her, "and his pager number." Lissa added the second number under the first. "Try either of those."

"Thank you, Aunt Enid."

"Are you all right?"

"I'm scared," Lissa admitted. "Did Hanson hurt you?"

"I'm still in one piece…and grateful to hear your voice."

After saying good-bye, Lissa hung up the phone and redialed, waiting impatiently as the sounds of buzzing sounded in her ear. The hour was very late. The ringing stopped.

"Yes," a male voice said.

Lissa swallowed her gasp of dismay and slammed the receiver into its cradle.

She remembered all too well the dispassionate voice of the man with the papers.

"Are you all right?" Katey asked.

Lissa knew she had lost all her color, but she nodded. That man…she closed her mind to the thought of him.

Lissa redialed, leaving her name and number with a pager service. Minutes later, the Vander Lynden's telephone gave a shrill demand. Silently requesting permission from the couple watching her, Lissa answered.

"*Lissa!*"

Brent's voice sounded…wonderful. "The very same," Lissa replied with a sober flick of humor, adding a fervent, brief prayer of thanksgiving to the God who supplies so richly. Tears began to form in her eyes.

"Where are you?" Brent continued.

"I don't know," she said, beginning to cry and laugh at

the same time. Lissa looked up at the bemused couple that stood watching her and asked, "Where am I?"

Pastor Louis gave her an address that she passed on to Brent.

"Stay where you are," Brent instructed. "Don't go anywhere. I'm already on my way."

– 25 –

A scant hour later headlights flickered through the row of pines protecting the front lawn. Twin beams of light glowed into the Vander Lynden house as a car turned into the driveway. Lissa jumped up from the sofa and rushed out the front door. Brent's car had barely stopped before he was out of it. Throwing herself into his arms, Lissa could feel Brent steady himself against the thrust of her weight.

"I am so sorry," Brent whispered. "What you must have gone through. I was helpless to do anything except try to keep you alive as long as possible," Brent shook with emotion, "and then I couldn't get back."

"It's all right," Lissa assured him. "I understand."

For a long moment they stood silently, each drawing security from the other's embrace. Lissa had not realized how dependent she had become on him—not merely for her life, but because...because he was...Brent.

Brent's grip lessened. His face was pale and gaunt in the bluish glow of the street light. Lissa could see the coarse

163

shadow of his beard...and a strange, possessive light in his darkened eyes. "I keep thanking God you're safe," Brent said. "It's like all my bad dreams are becoming reality, and I can't stop them from happening."

Lissa laid her hand against the side of his face. The stubble pricked her tender fingertips. Bandages protected her palms. "I praise God right now for the sight of you. You don't know how scared I've been."

His fingers gently cupped hers, inspecting the bandages.

"She scraped them," Louis said before Brent could comment. The Vander Lyndens came toward Brent and Lissa. "Katey cleaned them up as best she could, but a doctor might want to check them out. There was a pretty deep slice in one palm, but we don't think it'll need stitches."

Katey carried a jacket. It looked worn about the edges, even in the uncertain light, but as Lissa accepted it she knew it would be warm. It seemed she was constantly changing possession of clothing in the attempt to keep warm. She was grateful for how the Lord provided her needs.

Brent introduced himself, saying, "Thank you for what you've done for Lissa. I realize this must all seem confusing, but for your own safety—and Lissa's—I would ask that you not discuss these events with anyone."

Pastor Louis's broad face studied the couple before him. "I've seen some strange things in the ministry," he said, "but never anything quite like this. It gives a body something to think about." The corners of his lips lifted as his brows mimicked the action. "I don't know the task you two people have to do, but whatever it is, you can be certain Katey and I will be praying about it for you."

"Can we pray now?" Lissa asked.

Pastor Vander Lynden's smile broadened. He reached for his wife's hand, and Brent's. The tips of Lissa's fingers tightened on Katey's as Katey reached toward her, and the four of them formed a circle on the darkened lawn of the Vander Lynden's home.

"Our God and Father," Pastor Louis started. "I give glory and praise for who you are—the Creator of the heavens and the earth. I praise you for your wisdom in knowing what is best. And I praise you for your mercies in the events of our lives.

"Tonight we have seen the mercy of your protective hand over Lissa. You have never said we would understand all you do, but by faith we accept the working of your will. I ask now that you protect Brent and Lissa as they complete the work you are directing them to do. Give them the wisdom to make the right decisions, and the protection they need to do it safely. This we ask in your Son Jesus' name."

All echoed Pastor Louis's fervent, "Amen!"

Brent and Lissa hurried to leave. Lissa looked back once, briefly, as she got in Brent's car. She wished she had more time to get to know these people. Later, perhaps...when all of this was over...she and Brent would be able to come back.

Brent had barely started the car before Lissa asked, "What happened? Where did you go?"

"I was unavoidably detained," Brent said in a dry tone, touching the tips of his fingers gingerly to the crown of his head. "I have a lump the size of a melon and a cut three inches long. It bled profusely. The doctor went into a fit when I refused to stay at the hospital." One brow shifted upward as Brent glanced at Lissa. "Hanson flew into a rage when we disagreed over a minor detail. He struck me— must have thought I was dead because he left me where I lay. By all rights I should have been...or at the very least unconscious for the next two weeks. I informed the Organization just before you called. Hanson's employment contract is terminated."

"What about Detective Bendar?"

Brent looked her direction. "This case is falling apart at the seams. Sidney's in the hospital. Someone...was quite efficient. He hasn't regained consciousness."

"Marvin Frost," Lissa said.

"I suspected that possibility after I got your note." He removed a crumpled envelope from his pocket and handed it to Lissa. It was the second one she had written.

Lissa said, "He stole the file on Senator Craymore."

"A decoy," Brent replied. "I have the original hidden safely away."

"So much for my efforts to hide it," Lissa said, then began to relay the events since Brent left her in Hanson's room, adding, "I'm afraid for Karl. Senator Craymore's defeats are doing something to him. I told him about his wife leaving. I think something happened to his mind. He went...cold. Deadly. The look in his eyes...reminded me of a rattlesnake I saw once. Sinister. Chilling. Detached."

Grimly, Brent flipped open a panel between their seats and tapped a number of buttons before lifting the mobile telephone receiver to his ear.

Listening to Brent's end of the conversation, Lissa suspected he was speaking with the same man she had spoken to earlier. Brent requested confirmation of additional security for Karl. After a few additional comments, adding a phrase regarding Lissa's condition and requesting a search for Marvin Frost, Brent hung up.

The sky lightened with a faint suggestion of gray. A weary sigh overcame Lissa. "I'm so sick of all this," she said. "I want to sleep in my own bed, shower, wear my own clothes, run my company, and be...a photographer." She paused. "How do you stay in this business, Brent?"

"It's not a perfect society we're living in. Someone needs to do the job."

He was right. But, "Why you?"

166

"Why not me?"

"You could get hurt—you *did* get hurt."

"Where would you be if I hadn't been there?"

Lissa sighed again, understanding where he was coming from. "I am grateful you're willing to take the risks involved."

"It is a dangerous business," he conceded, adding, "But it's what I do."

Lissa's hand reached to touch his. "I'm afraid for you. I found...you are special to me...and it...makes me afraid... knowing you do this type of work for a living."

The smile he gave her was weary and a bit determined. His fingers curled tenderly around hers. The look in his eyes caused Lissa to wonder at the words she'd said. They were true, but she never thought she would ever say those words to Brent.

Lifting her hand, Brent touched his lips, ever so softly, to her knuckles. Lissa's fingers tightened. In her heart she marveled over the emotion caused by this man...and wondered what the Lord had in store for the two of them.

With her free hand, Lissa toyed with the corner of the envelope Brent handed her, then smoothed it across her knee. On the front, in the light of dawn, under where she had written Brent's name, Lissa noticed Brent's forceful scrawl spelling out 527 12th St.

527 12th.

5 27 12.

Lissa drew a slow breath of growing astonishment. Lifting the envelope, she stared at it, disbelieving the simplicity she had neglected to see.

Why hadn't she seen it before now? How could she have been so dull?

Her fingers tightened on his, "Brent...."

"What is it?"

167

"I know what the key is for."

Brent's eyes darkened, points of blue glittering with intensity. The first rays of sunrise broke the horizon. "You do?"

Lissa grinned, repeating, "I know what the key is for."

– 26 –

"It was the numbers that made me see," Lissa said, raising the envelope. "The numbers and the fact that I use a combination to pick up Karl's mail at the post office."

"What has that got to do with it?"

"Karl doesn't have his mail delivered at the apartment...but he still has the key to his *apartment* mailbox. It's perfect. The mailman never delivers there...and who would think to search that mailbox if his mail all arrives at the post office?"

Brent's intense expression met hers. "You have a point."

"I pray I'm right."

The remaining miles to Karl's passed in relative silence, both Brent and Lissa busy with their thoughts. Lissa wondered over the subtle genius Karl had used...then wondered about Karl himself. She wanted to see him, to be certain he was all right.

When Karl's apartment complex came into view, Brent whipped his car into the first open spot he saw. Cutting across the grounds, the two of them rushed to the building door and yanked it open. Lissa paused to catch her breath just inside the entry. Along one side of the entry were two rows of mailboxes.

"Where's the key?" Brent asked.

Lissa stood still. "Senator Craymore has it."

Brent's face went blank.

"I've got an idea," Lissa said. Grabbing Brent's hand, they hurried around the corner to Jeremy's apartment.

Eventually Jeremy answered Lissa's insistent ringing. He was bleary-eyed and rumpled and a bit surprised to see the couple standing on his doorstep. "Lissa...." Jeremy yawned, then apologized. He scratched his thatch of tousled hair, trying to rake it into place. "What's up?"

"Do you have a spare key to Karl's mailbox?"

"Sure. I have spare keys to all the mailboxes. Why?"

"Can you bring it?" Lissa asked. "We need to take a look inside the box."

There were three boxes without names, but Jeremy knew which one belonged to Karl. He inserted his key, twisted it to the right, and swung the door open.

A deep breath of disbelieving thankfulness escaped from Lissa's lips. Her eyes shut for a half second as she breathed her fervent thanks. Inside, standing upright, were two innocent-seeming, tiny canisters. But Lissa knew they were not so innocent. Somehow the film those canisters contained had been the cause of Karl's shooting, Lissa's abduction, and Brent and Sidney Bendar's injuries. They had to be the pictures Karl said he was going to take. Who knew what else might happen...had happened because of the secrets they held?

Lissa snatched the rolls of film. She clutched them in her fist. The mailbox door snapped shut.

"I'll take those," Brent said.

"Brent, I realize you have all the authority in the world

to override me, but I'm asking you to please let me develop them. You have to let me. I have to know the truth."

Brent watched Lissa, his expression tired, resigned. "Let's go," he said and they left.

By the time they made it to the McIntyre family home, the early sunrise had clouded to wintry gray. Brent had agreed to the home when Lissa said she had a darkroom there and refused to endanger any of her employees by their presence at Created Images's lab.

"I need to make a phone call," Brent said, entering the house behind Lissa.

"Through the house to the kitchen," Lissa told him. "I'm going upstairs to the attic. My darkroom's there."

"Lissa," Brent caught her as she turned. Lissa stopped, captured by his touch...and the look in his eyes. "Please trust me. No matter what happens I will protect you. I will never deliberately hurt you." His eyes glittered with points of gray. "There is so much I wish I could explain."

"You will," she said. "When you can. I know that."

He studied her for a space of time, then turned away. For a moment, Lissa watched him move. He looked tired. Pulling his gun from its holster, Brent inspected the loads...then disappeared from view.

Lissa hung her coat on a hook on the back of the darkroom door and removed the canisters from her pocket before locating an apron and tying it on. She scanned the shelves. There was enough of what she needed.

While she worked, Lissa's mind wandered over the events of the past weeks. She recognized her growing attraction toward Brent and wondered if this was the man the Lord had chosen for her. She had to admit it was what she would have originally considered an unlikely coupling...but her feelings toward Brent had grown to more than a passing interest. She cared about him. A lot.

Stripping off excess water, Lissa held the black and white

171

negatives up to the light. The first roll looked like loading docks, crates, and boxes. The second contained a myriad of shots, including cars, broken windows, old buildings, and—what was this? Some indistinct photos of what could only be people.

Grabbing a blow dryer, Lissa set it on low and carefully dried the negatives. She snipped the last six exposures from the end of the roll and laid the others aside.

Starting with the first negative, Lissa exposed and developed a print. The first was fuzzy, the forms barely identifiable. The second was better. There were five—no, six men in the picture...and she recognized Senator Craymore even under the subtle red glow of the safe light. Lissa clipped the wet sheet of developed paper up by its corner so she could study the print. It appeared to be an indoor shot of a large room—warehouse type. The men were standing in a group. Senator Craymore was the only man who directly faced the camera.

The next picture was close to the same. The people had shifted and a briefcase could be seen. Lissa hurried to expose the fourth print. She dropped the exposed paper into the tray of developer and waited, gently rocking the tray to agitate the developing fluid across the surface of the print. Slowly, forms began to take shape.

It appeared to be an argument. Two men faced off. She recognized the man with the papers from Senator Craymore's home, and another she did not know, each in a position and with a facial expression indicating their anger.

Snaring the strip of negatives, Lissa thrust them into the negative carrier, securing the next to the last shot into place. Lissa altered the lights accordingly and turned on the enlarging lamp, adjusting the focus to make an 8 x 10 enlargement of...the attempted murderer's face!

It was obvious even in the negative caricature of the frozen moment in time that this man held a gun, pointed directly at the camera. Lissa's heart thumped. This was the person who shot Karl.

A minute later, Lissa watched the exposed print rock in the developing tray. Features began to emerge. She wanted to be certain—to have proof that Hanson did it. She knew it had to be him.

Lissa studied the face, watching as details etched themselves into the paper.

Realization came slowly, disbelievingly as her head slowly shook in dismayed horror. She lifted the dripping print from the tray.

Staring back was the tight-lipped, grim face of Detective Brent Jamison.

– 27 –

A cry of horrified dismay filled the small room.
"Brent?"

No! Brent was undercover, but even in that capacity, he could not have shot Karl. Not for any reason. She could not believe that. She would not believe that.

All the same, Lissa's hands shook as one at a time she made blowups of the other faces. Besides Senator Craymore, one of the men was Hanson and the man with the papers. Another man looked vaguely familiar. She definitely did not recognize the other person. And then there was Brent.

She stopped.

Lord..Brent didn't really shoot Karl...did he?

Why hadn't Brent told her who shot Karl? Certainly his reasoning was not that he wanted her to find the film. What difference would that make?...Except he might assume she wouldn't help him otherwise.

Unthinkable doubts were beginning to seep in. Her heart wrenched within her. Photographs don't lie.

But...do they tell the entire truth?

Lissa placed all the photographs in a manila envelope.

The impact of Brent's possible betrayal was difficult to understand, but the evidence...was...it was purely circumstantial! Lissa raked her nails back through her hair and paused. Is this why Karl had said not to trust anyone? He must have recognized Brent from somewhere. Is that why Karl wouldn't go to the police?...Because the police were involved just as deeply as....

Lissa made a sound of denial.

Not Brent!

She stopped.

What if Brent *had* been the one to shoot Karl?

Could it have been an accident?

Lissa fought the essence of fraud that permeated the entire affair. She denied the possibility that she could be deceived by someone she was beginning to...to care about very deeply. No, Brent was not capable of coldbloodedly, deliberately murdering another human being. She would not...could not...believe it.

Snatching at her coat, Lissa picked up the envelope and opened the door...and suddenly felt sick. Her color faded. Her heart pounded deep and heavy in her chest.

Brent's lips were thin, drawn to a fine line. He blinked, the color of his eyes glittering. A sound came from the shadows behind him and Lissa saw another man...one of the unidentified men from the photographs. Voice tight, holding out his free hand, Brent said, "I'll take those."

Lissa stared.

"Now," he ordered. Lissa handed the envelope to him and Brent said, "Let's go."

The stairway yawned before her. Lissa's mind spun in circles, trying to decide what to do, what to believe.

She did not know anymore.

Lord, if Brent has deceived me about who and what he

*is, help me not to be bitter. I don't understand your thinking,
but I trust your judgment. Only you know what happens
from moment to moment. Somehow you're in control. But I
need your help so desperately!*

They walked outside; the still air had a cutting edge. Lissa
slipped into the coat she had grabbed. "Don't try anything,"
she was warned by the man with Brent. Brent remained
forebodingly silent.

Lissa was surprised to see there were now three cars in
the driveway. She was given a directing push toward the
parked cars. Three men emerged from the last car. Lissa
swallowed her gasp of dismay. Senator Craymore and the
paper man and one other. Now five of the six men in the
photographs were here, and she was not under any delusion
as to what could happen to her.

Believing they possessed the negatives and only
photographs of their meeting, Lissa was the only one, besides
Karl, who could testify against them.

How could she possibly get out of this?

She chanced a look at Brent. He did not look at her. What
would he do? Doubts pummeled her.

Senator Craymore came to within a few feet of Lissa.
"You led us around quite a bit," he smiled tightly when
Brent handed over Karl's pictures, "but I see it's paid off."

A sudden sharp taste came to Lissa's mouth. Was Brent...
truly one of them? She wanted to deny it, but he had
passed the photographs Karl had hidden to a...a
thief...and...and....

"How could you do that?" Staring at Brent's stiff face,
Lissa could not stop the words that began pouring from her
mouth. "I *trusted* you. Are you really a hit man?" She
touched his arm, snagged the material of his coat. "Is that
it? Is it your own special form of a mini-mafia I'm seeing
here?" Her eyes glittered with emotion, her voice wavered
with betrayal. "Why do you do it? What's in it for you?"

Senator Craymore chuckled. "Money, of course," he said. Brent removed Lissa's fingers, and Lissa pulled away from his touch.

Lissa's gaze narrowed on the senator. "What are you covering up?"

He shrugged and pursed his lips—a quick gesture. "Besides eliminating leaks in my system? Trafficking in miscellaneous profitable items, bribery, fraud. I'm afraid my hands are quite dirty....And I couldn't possibly permit you back on the streets after being so frank with you. That would be bad for my career and I have, shall we say, high aspirations."

"Are you going to kill me like you tried to kill Karl?" Lissa asked.

"It's important that I wrap up loose ends...and you and your boyfriend are just a couple of those irritating threads we need to snip off and tidy up."

"You have a very low estimate of people, don't you, Senator Craymore?"

The smile the man gave her was unpleasant and condescending. "Those who accidentally or intentionally stumble on events that are none of their business are simply eliminated."

"If you're going to put an end to my life I'd at least like to know what for."

"Power," the senator said, his handsome face lighting with his thoughts. He added, "I could probably tack greed to that, but I prefer calling it, 'The enjoyment of the better things in life'."

"At the expense of people's *lives*?"

"Reality be known, I have nothing against you or your boyfriend," the senator said. "However, both of you were in the wrong place at the wrong time." Abruptly the senator changed the flow of discussion. His look focused on the man with Brent. "You know what you have to do."

177

"No, I'll do it." This came from Brent.

Lissa stared at him.

The senator's glance flicked over Brent. "I've had my doubts where you've been concerned lately, Brent, but I can see I was mistaken." He made a sharp movement. "Be quick about it. I want this business finished." The senator returned to his car with his companions.

Other than the color of his face, Brent showed no emotion. His skin was sallow, drawn. The flecks of gray and blue in his eyes contrasted with the brown. He took Lissa's arm and said, "This way."

"Where are you taking me?"

The other man followed a few steps back. Brent stopped, turned. "I will take care of this myself."

Leaves crackled beneath their feet as Brent led her toward the trees. Voices drifted toward her from the cars, audible in the still biting air.

Lissa knew her face was pale, but she raised her chin when Brent released her arm. She was not surprised when he withdrew his pistol and pointed it at her chest.

There was an indescribable look in Brent's eyes.

She remembered his directions to trust him—*explicitly, without question.*

But he shot Karl.

I would never deliberately hurt you.

Locking her eyes on his, she asked, "Did you shoot Karl?"

"No." The word was abrupt, soft, bitten off. "I'm sorry, Lissa."

The words came from somewhere beyond the roaring in her ears. She saw his hand raise the gun, his finger squeeze the trigger, heard the explosion of sound.

A blow struck her chest. Waves of darkness danced before her eyes.

In the distance Lissa could hear the sound of police sirens. Too late....

– 28 –

The first thing Lissa was aware of as she struggled to lift herself out of the depth of darkness she had sunk into was that it hurt to breathe.

She heard herself groan.

A numbish ache pulsed through most of her body...and she found she was unable to move. She was on her back. Lissa fought to open her eyes. Her mouth was cottony with a brassy taste. She tried to swallow with only moderate success.

Able to force her eyelids to an opened slit, Lissa attempted to right her blurred vision...and realized as fuzzy objects endeavored to form distinct lines that she was no longer outside. Her head shook as threads of darkness threatened to overtake her senses again.

Where was she?

Her eyelids dropped as memories tried to swirl over her.

Brent...staring at her, grim and ashen, holding....

The gun!

A cry of denial filled the room as Lissa tried to escape the sound of an explosion echoing in her head...the slamming thud against her chest...the wail of police sirens.

Lissa's eyes shot open and she stared wildly about her. She lifted a hand to her chest. A woman was beside her, uttering words that made no sense.

Her hands shoved at a blanket, fumbling with the front of a gown, fighting the woman who was trying to restrain her.

There was no bloody wound...no bandages....

She was not shot!

"How?" Lissa croaked.

Her vision spun. Her head felt like it was stuffed with cotton.

She tried to focus on the woman—her white uniform finally registered. A nurse! Lissa's hand snared a wrist.

Lissa breathed in slowly, her senses whirling. There was bruising...pricked skin abrasions...from the impact of whatever struck her...but not death.

"You were drugged," Lissa heard through the gray fog. "Detective Jamison shot you with a tranquili...."

Drugged.

Brent...did—Lissa fought the sinking darkness that threatened to overtake her—protect her...like...he'd promised.

Something woke her. What, Lissa was not certain, but something. A tired sigh came from her lips—a small one. She was on her side. Dull, insistent pain pulsated throughout her body. Her mouth twitched. She tried to swallow, then lick her lips. Dry.

Another sigh, this time stronger. Lissa pushed at the blanket that had been placed over her. Her eyes opened just enough to peer straight ahead. Sunlight leaked past the drawn edges of lined draperies. A light was on low above and behind her.

Sleepily, Lissa refocused. From the look of it, she was in

a hospital room. Private. Muffled sounds of hospital personnel at work seeped through the closed door.

Shifting again, Lissa stretched. Her body objected. Easing off her side and onto her back, Lissa took in the full sweep of the sizable room...and spied Brent, sleeping, slouched in a chair pushed into the corner near the head of the bed. His clothes were rumpled, his hair in need of combing, his unshaved face haggard, and even in sleep there was a disturbed frown creasing his brow.

Lissa watched the man with mixed feelings. So much had happened. He had not shot Karl. She knew that without question now. And he had not tried to kill her. He had— she realized with a start—saved her life.

She lay quietly, studying him...realizing that she felt strongly for this man...even...loved him.

Loved him.

She almost laughed—a sober, dry sound in her mind—at the oddity of it...and was amazed by the thought that God had brought them together. She knew that now. Never had she thought she would meet a man like this by playing a game of Resistance.

No. Not by playing. The pain throughout her body attested to the fact that what she had experienced was no game.

Lissa looked back at Brent. She had so many questions to ask him...later...after they both rested, when they could be alone and talk openly.

Her door cracked open. A nurse peeked into the room. Lissa laid her finger across her lips and pointed toward Brent.

A silent nod came from the pleasant-faced woman who quietly edged through the doorway. She whispered, "Did you sleep well?"

Lissa nodded, then added a shrug. The way she felt, she could sleep another three days before she wanted to face the real world again. Whatever Brent had shot at her had done an effective job.

"How long has he been there?" Lissa whispered.

"Except for when the doctors examined him or you, the entire time you've been here. He was beside himself with worry about the shock you went through. The doctors finally threatened to hospitalize him if he didn't calm down. Confidentially," her brows raised, "he needed the tranquilizer the doctors gave him."

After tending to her duties, the nurse said, "We got a call from upstairs a few minutes ago. You have a friend asking to see you."

Lissa stared at the woman. "Karl?"

"Would you like to see him?"

"*Would* I? Yes, I'd like that very much."

"I'll bring a wheelchair for you."

"Don't bother," Lissa said, continuing to whisper as she sat up and pushed her covers away. "I'll walk."

"That might not be wise yet, Miss McIntyre."

"I'm not an invalid," Lissa said, but not unkindly. "I'm stiff and sore and need to walk the kinks out. If you want to come along to keep an eye on me, great, but don't bother with the wheelchair because I am outta here."

When her weight hit her feet, Lissa bit her lip to keep the protesting groan that surged forward from becoming a reality. Getting a wheelchair might be a better idea, but it would take time, and Lissa did not intend to wait. She wanted to see Karl now, to assure herself that he was coherent and improving.

Lissa glanced at Brent's inert form and debated on whether to wake him and let him know where she was going.

She decided against it. He needed sleep, too. Besides, she would have a nurse with her, and there were policemen on Karl's floor.

Drawing a breath, Lissa pushed at her hair, knowing she looked as rumpled as Brent. She would like to trade this gown for a pair of jeans, but she settled for the

182

robe at the end of her bed instead.

While Lissa's nurse informed the desk she was going upstairs with Lissa, Lissa waited impatiently. People moved about them—visitors, doctors, nurses. Lissa walked toward the dual set of elevators down the hall and punched the correct button. A red, triangular arrow lit, indicating the upward direction.

When a soft dong sounded, Lissa watched the doors part and stepped on with the nurse scurrying right behind her.

"You don't waste any time, do you?" the nurse asked in a mildly dry tone of voice.

"If you have other things you need to do, it isn't really necessary for you to follow along with me. I won't be gone long."

"We've had strict instructions where you're concerned. Between Detective Jamison and Dr. Bailey, we've been told in no uncertain terms that someone is to know where you are at all times."

"I'm surprised there were no police guarding my door."

"There are still two men upstairs. What are you? Security secrets?"

Lissa looked at the woman. A smile touched the corners of her lips. "Hardly," she replied.

The elevator stopped to let on two more passengers who disembarked at the next level up. Alone again, Lissa and the nurse rode silently, watching floor numbers flash. The elevator slowed for another stop. Lissa saw they were shy of the floor she wanted by one stop. The doors slid back. She looked...and gasped!

The instant, wicked grin of Hanson gleamed back!

Lissa lunged to punch the "close" button.

She did not make it in time.

Hanson's fist flew out to jam the doors open. A deep chuckle sounded in the man's throat. "My mistake could not have been more opportune," he stated. "Step on out,

Miss McIntyre. I may not have gotten the correct floor for Karello, but this is better—*much* better."

"No way," Lissa replied with flat finality. "There's not a thing you can do here without getting caught. You'd better give up. I'm not going anywhere with you."

"Then," Hanson replied matter-of-factly, "your nurse friend dies here."

The woman beside Lissa blanched. Her open, frightened stare fastened itself in horror on the small gun Hanson unobtrusively lifted from his pocket.

"Don't be a hero at the expense of another life, Miss McIntyre." A peculiar look of exultation lit Hanson's eyes. "You can come along now, too," he said, indicating the nurse with a jerk of his head.

Hanson's hand slid back to his pocket as the two women made their way off the elevator. Another couple, unaware of the drama being acted out in front of them, walked by and went up with the elevator.

Lissa took hold of the trembling nurse's arm as they made their way, according to directions, down the hall a short distance to an enclosed stairwell. Praying, her mind worked at the same time, trying to come up with an idea—any idea that would help this trembling, silent woman beside her...and protect the rest of the people in the building as well. Who knew what Hanson had planned?

Lissa's heart pounded heavily in her chest.

The door whooshed open and shut with a determined snick behind the three people. The sound echoed up and down the stairwell.

"Down," Hanson ordered.

Vibrations from their steps bounced against the walls of their surroundings. Turning at a landing, Lissa looked out a window that faced a view of the city. So many people. And not one knew her danger.

Hanson was one step behind the two women. He carried

his weapon openly now.

"How do you plan to get away with this?" Lissa asked.

"I may not plan to get away with anything, Miss McIntyre."

The words stopped Lissa in her tracks. Her nurse bumped into her and the two steadied one another.

"What did you say?" Lissa asked. Her question reverberated against the walls.

"All I plan to do is make you and Karello and Jamison suffer."

"You're going to ruin all our lives, including this woman's, just for the sake of revenge? *Why?*"

"Get moving!" Hanson growled.

The nurse snatched at Lissa's arm, dragging her forward and down. Her pale face was drawn, her eyes nervously begging Lissa to follow directions.

"If revenge is all you're after," Lissa continued, "you won't need this woman. Let her go. She hasn't done anything to you."

Hanson did not answer. Their footsteps shuffled down, the sound loud in Lissa's ears. Beside her, the nurse breathed harshly. The grip the woman had on Lissa sent an intensified ache up Lissa's arm.

They passed another door. Down...another landing and window. Above them, Lissa heard a door open and close.

"Keep moving," Hanson hissed. "And keep your mouths shut."

A voice hummed a tune. Steps tapped their way downward. Lissa moved on, the pounding in her chest accelerating.

Now was the time.

Dare she threaten someone else's life?

The sound of footsteps came closer. Ahead, a door stood waiting. Beside her, the nurse looked ghastly, as if she were about to faint.

Lissa chanced a glance up as the new footsteps slowed. A portion of a central wall blocked her view. The man's humming continued, louder.

The door was three steps away. Only three steps.

"Howdy, folks!" a man's voice boomed. "Great day, ain't it?" The rolling sounds thundered down the echoing recesses.

Lissa's gaze flicked back as the man spoke...in time to see a huge, muscular arm raise to flatten Hanson between the shoulder blades.

Hanson's breath expelled in one great rush. He staggered against the wall.

The door below exploded open.

"Get down!" Brent yelled at Lissa. He scrambled to the side of the landing, spinning to steady his aim at Hanson.

Lissa threw herself against the nurse, dragging the woman the last few steps. With a mighty jerk and shove, she thrust the woman through the doorway...and heard the angry crack and retort of a weapon being fired.

Another.

Silence.

Lissa hugged the nurse close, the sobbing woman shaking, hysterical. A police officer was already at the door, weapon drawn.

"Please," Lissa said to a man—a doctor. "Take her." Faces peered from around corners and doorways. The doctor's eyes were huge.

A man appeared at the stairwell door. Brent's drawn figure came through. He replaced his weapon in his shoulder holster.

Lissa threw her arms around him. Brent's arms rested carefully, gently around her...and tightened.

"We'll need a doctor," Lissa heard him say. Weariness hung on each word.

– 29 –

Lissa and Brent strode through the sliding glass doors of the hospital entrance. Lissa's heels tapped the linoleum in firm, even strides. Her hand rested comfortably in Brent's warm grasp.

More than a week had passed since Lissa's ordeal at the hands of Senator Craymore and Hanson. Hanson's injured hand would heal, although the medical reports stated it would not retain the flexibility it once had before Brent's shot shattered the thumb and the tendons in his hand. At this point Hanson was facing charges of attempted murder and assault against both Karl and Brent. More charges were pending.

The senator was in custody without bond. The charges against him were numerous and, if convicted, Walter Craymore stood to spend the majority of the rest of his life in prison. The police had arrived moments after Brent was forced to act out Lissa's fatal shooting in order to protect her life.

187

Key figures associated with Senator Craymore had been arrested. All the photographs and negatives were recovered safely in spite of Senator Craymore's last-minute efforts to destroy them. Due to the sensitive nature of some of Senator Craymore's exploits, Karl and Lissa were still under police protection, but for the most part, life was back to normal.

Olivia Craymore had proven to be a strong woman. In spite of public opinion, she was standing beside her husband in an attempt to show her support for the man she loved. Perhaps only Lissa knew the difficulty and pain behind that action. Especially since Lissa knew how desperately Olivia Craymore hated what her husband had done.

Brent's own reason for being involved with the entire case, he admitted, was originally due to the fact that Walter Craymore had been instrumental in destroying his father's health by involving him in questionable business practices. Roland Jamison had been trapped by Walter Craymore's devious tactics and deceit. The desire to avenge his father had originally spurred Brent on. Now he was grateful the ordeal was coming to an end.

The elevator stopped smoothly at Karl's floor. Brent and Lissa stepped out. Brent's fingers tightened on Lissa's, and she returned the pressure as they moved down the hall.

In the past week, Karl's health had improved greatly, almost miraculously, the doctors said. Once the infection was conquered, Karl became coherent and nearly his old self. Although the doctors were advising otherwise, Karl was already insisting it was time for him to get back to work.

The officer outside Karl's room recognized Brent and Lissa as they moved toward the door.

Brent knocked and pushed the door open.

"Lissa!" Karl exclaimed. "And Brent...come in!"

No longer tormented by his injury, Karl's eyes reflected the mischievous gleam he normally wore. His beard had been trimmed and his hair cut. Beside Karl stood a woman, her fingers entwined with his. Olive-skinned with dark hair down to her waist, the woman's large, brown eyes focused on Lissa and Brent. She was beautiful.

"I've had a superb surprise. Do you remember," Karl continued, his hand lifting, beckoning them, "before this got started, my message on your answering machine about the wonderful news I wanted to tell you? This is Mara...my wonderful news. And we've got something to share."

"Tell me," Lissa replied, answering the woman's ready smile with one of her own. "What news can there possibly be that would excite you so much?"

"We're getting married," Mara answered in a soft voice. It was lightly accented, her English measured.

"Isn't that fantastic?" Karl inserted. "She said, 'Yes'."

Lissa gave the slender woman a heartfelt smile and a warm hug. "I think it's wonderful. Congratulations."

"I feel I owe you a great debt of gratitude," Mara replied. "Karl has been telling me how the two of you saved his life."

Lissa's look took in everyone around her. "I think we can safely say it was God who preserved us all." Mara and Karl both nodded. Lissa added, "I wish you both great happiness together."

"You will be in our wedding?" Mara asked. "We will marry here."

"Of course."

"Brent, too," Karl added. "I can think of no better man to be my best man."

Brent gave a dry chuckle. "Is that flattery or what?"

"Great!" Karl said. "I take that as an affirmative. We're making plans now. As soon as the doctors spring me, we're going to get serious about setting a date."

"Speaking of dates," Brent inserted, "I have a date with a very special lady for dinner out. If what my stomach says is any indication," he consulted his watch, "—and it is—it's way past time to have some food. You may get yours on a tray, but we normal people still have to fend for ourselves."

Karl smiled soberly as he said, "As soon as I get out of here, I owe Lissa a meal, too—at Ricardo's. Let's make it a foursome."

Lissa looked at Brent who nodded his agreement. "It's a deal," she said.

On the ride back to the lobby, Lissa and Brent were quiet. Brent's fingers laced with Lissa's. She liked the feel of his thumb moving across the back of her hand. The fingers of her free hand absentmindedly reached for a gold circle dangling from a chain around her neck. When her fingers couldn't feel it, she dropped his hand. Eventually the police would return it to her; they had retrieved it from Senator Craymore, and she intended to give it to Mara.

Brent said, "Pastor Vander Lynden has a compelling love for God, doesn't he?" Lissa smiled in silent agreement. "This morning's service really hit home. I needed to hear what he said about the reality of true forgiveness. It helped me remember Christ's loving sacrifice and what He has done for me. And Pastor Vander Lynden was so willing to spend time in prayer with me." He sighed, a satisfied sound. "I feel...clean now that I've asked God to forgive me for taking matters into my own hands and turning my back on Him."

"I'm so glad you're growing closer to the Lord again," Lissa said, squeezing his hand.

"Me, too," Brent said, adding a moment later, "and I'm really glad I'm getting to know you."

Lissa looked up into Brent's blue-flecked brown eyes to see the sweet seriousness lingering there.

Brent took Lissa's free hand in his. The look in his eyes captured her. "I thank God for bringing you into my life, Lissa. He knew I needed a straight-spoken, Christian woman to help me see what I had lost when I turned away from Him." A gentle smile hinted around the edges of his eyes

190

and at the corners of his mouth. "You do realize I've fallen in love with you?"

Lissa smiled, knowing her love filled her eyes for him to see.

Brent kissed Lissa, tenderly but firmly.

The elevator chimed and the doors slid back. A number of people stood waiting.

"Ready for that adventure in Greek dining I promised you?" he asked.

Lissa smiled, green eyes sparkling. "Haven't you had enough adventure lately?"